D0349982

BLANK PAGES

And Other Stories

BLANK PAGES

And Other Stories

Bernard MacLaverty

W. W. NORTON & COMPANY
Independent Publishers Since 1923

For information about permission to reproduce selections from this
book, write to Permissions, W. W. Norton & Company, Inc.,
500 Fifth Avenue, New York, NY 10110

For information about special discounts for bulk purchases, please
contact W. W. Norton Special Sales at specialsales@wwnorton.com or
800-233-4830

Manufacturing by Lakeside Book Company

Library of Congress Cataloging-in-Publication Data

Names: MacLaverty, Bernard, author.
Title: Blank pages : and other stories / Bernard MacLaverty.
Description: First American edition. |
New York : W. W. Norton & Company, 2022.
Identifiers: LCCN 2021037010 | ISBN 9780393881592 (hardcover)
| ISBN 9780393881608 (epub)
Subjects: LCGFT: Short stories.
Classification: LCC PR6063.A2474 B58 2022 | DDC 823/.914—dc23
LC record available at https://lccn.loc.gov/2021037010

W. W. Norton & Company, Inc., 500 Fifth Avenue,
New York, N.Y. 10110
www.wwnorton.com

W. W. Norton & Company Ltd., 15 Carlisle Street, London W1D 3BS

1 2 3 4 5 6 7 8 9 0

For Madeline, always and everywhere

CONTENTS

A LOVE PICTURE

Belfast 1940

S he set the egg in its eggcup. No sooner had she sat
down than she had to get up and go to the kitchen
for a spoon. There was a step down, which she took in
her stride. The small apostle spoon she used for eating an
egg from its shell was in the cutlery drawer and she rattled
around until she found it.

She was not the slightest bit interested in food but knew
she should eat. To keep herself going. Since it happened,
there was a strange feeling in her stomach all the time.
Frank. It was the crying – its volume filling her insides.
Her only son. Great gulps of air inflating her. Other times
she felt wrung out – emptied of everything.

She didn't set the table. Just put things on a folded
tablecloth to deaden the sound. Of plates, cutlery. The
teapot had its own cork mat to avoid bleaching the wood.
She sat and sliced the top off her egg. If the wireless was
anything to go by, eggs too would be rationed soon
enough.

It was the sheer relentlessness of the thoughts. There was nothing between them. End to end, thinking of the same thing. Adding a little each time. Rarely subtracting from it. Enlarging the tragedy in her mind. Adding the incidentals. Little things. What shirt had he been wearing? Had she ironed it? There was one had seen better days – gone to threads. But he'd had a fondness for it and she mended it in such a way he'd get another year out of it. He'd only been away three days when it happened.

Tapping the salt cellar with her finger, she put a little salt on her egg and took a spoonful. Then more salt when the yolk showed. She realised she was crying again. Thinking about Frank's shirts. She thought she'd cried every last drop out of her. Between times, she'd tried not to think. But it was difficult not to think. It was like trying not to see when your eyes were open. The thoughts came and came. Were unstoppable. She closed her eyes and shuddered.

She had gone through grief many years before, when her husband Paddy had died. He'd been from a seafaring Belfast family and after the First War he was involved in shipping troops here, there and everywhere. He died in Halifax, Nova Scotia. Of a heart attack. It might as well be the other side of the world. It *was* the other side of the world. That was when she gave up praying. She went to church occasionally, but inside herself she was no longer present. A woman doesn't recover from something like that, being widowed in her mid-thirties.

She took a handkerchief from her sleeve and blew her nose. Taking control. She scraped a little egg white from the inside of the shell and put it in her mouth. It tasted of nothing. When things did not taste, there seemed little point in eating. She toasted bread at the fire on the end of a wire fork. Her brother had made it. Said it was telescopic. If the fire was too hot, you lengthened the fork and your hand didn't get scorched. The bread browned and filled the room with its smell. She was about to force herself to toast another bit when she heard the front door open. It was Letty. It's only me, she always said, halfway up the hall.

'It's only me.'

'It's yourself.'

'You're late at your tea tonight,' said Letty. Despite being dressed in her hat and overcoat, the younger woman sat down in the armchair by the fire. She was small but seemed to fill the chair with the orb of her pregnancy.

'I fell asleep earlier.'

'Aw, Aunt Gracie . . . '

'I get precious little sleep these nights – and what I do get is filled with such awful dreams – then you're dozing all day. Trying to make up for it.'

Letty nodded.

'Can the doctor not give you something? Barbiturates?'

'What do you think I am – a movie star?' said the older woman. 'I'd be afraid of getting hooked.'

'It'd only be for a short while. To get you through.'

'To get me through what? Lost at sea is for ever.'

Both sat silent for a while. Then Gracie spoke again.

'Barbiturates,' she said, 'they're better than the gas oven.'

'Aunt Gracie, don't you dare talk like that.'

'I'm sorry, love. I'm only kidding. I don't know what I'm saying these days.'

Gracie offered to toast her a slice of bread but Letty refused.

'I met Anne on the road today and she's coming with me. Instead of you.'

'That's nice. She's a good girl,' said Gracie.

'You don't mind me going?'

'Not at all, love. Why wouldn't you? Your friend Anne can do my job.'

'What?'

'Keep you awake. With her elbow.'

'I be that tired. And the place is so comfy.'

'Who's minding the wains?'

'Tommy. While he reads the paper.'

Both the women smiled. Gracie set the apostle spoon down.

'I find it hard to finish an egg these days.' She shook her head in exasperation. 'What's on?'

'Sure I never know what's on. It's my night out, that's enough.'

'Is it a love picture?'

'I've no idea,' Letty said. 'I think Cary Grant's in it.'

'Aw – that'll definitely be a love picture.'

Letty smiled. Too much of a smile. She joined her fingers across her stomach.

'What?' said the older woman. Letty continued to smile and drummed her fingers on her tummy.

'In Hollywood all it takes to have a baby is just the one kiss. Am I right?'

'Aye – they were real love stories. Where's it on?'

'The Capitol.'

'I hate that oul Lyceum,' said Gracie. 'There's just something about it. A smell. Overdoing the disinfectant. I like the Capitol better. Except for the double seats. I like those lover seats at the back in the Lyceum.'

Letty was agreeing and smiling.

'Are you sure . . . are you sure you won't come? Cary Grant?'

'Naw, love. It wouldn't feel right.'

Letty nodded.

'Any word?'

'No. Not a thing.'

Letty stood. She crossed from her chair and patted Gracie on the shoulder.

'Wrap up warm,' said her aunt.

When Letty had gone Gracie washed the dishes, not that there was much to wash. If she left them, they just accumulated in her mind. Sooner or later they had to be done. She was trying to maintain a regime of working as much as possible. To keep herself in the present. To be doing rather than thinking. The sounds of her work – clinking, running water, from both the tap and emptying from the sink. The little apostle spoon with the eggcup, upended to drain. Her teacup the same. She dried her hands on the roller towel on the back of the door and went upstairs to the bathroom. She had not been since lunchtime. The sound of running water always put her in the notion.

Afterwards she went into the bedroom and pulled the blackout curtains. There was enough light to see the grey patterns of frost on the inside of the windows. She checked by touching with her fingers. A cold sandpaper roughness. When the blinds met precisely, she turned on the light and looked at herself in the dressing-table mirror. It had helped stop her crying in the past – seeing herself from three different angles. The main mirror and the two narrow side mirrors. Like church windows.

She wondered about going into mourning. Somehow a black armband didn't seem enough. The things she had in her wardrobe were not at all suitable. When she opened the wardrobe doors there was a smell of mothballs. Difficult to judge the strength needed – between tainting her clothes and keeping the moths at bay. It was wool they were after. Like in her stone-coloured overcoat. Her only good suit was navy. White blouses. Comfy cardigans for warmth. And yet . . . and yet a black armband might be the answer. She stood looking around. Some day she would love to have a complete bedroom suite. Her chest of drawers and dressing table didn't match. For the first months of her baby's life, the top drawer of the dressing table had been slid out and used as a crib, padded with soft things – snug. For months it left a dark square hole in the dressing table – until she got a Moses basket. She felt the tears start again but this time they did not come.

She looked at herself. Too pale or was she just cold? Her hand touched the atomiser sitting on a doily on the dressing table. What about perfume? Was it right to wear perfume while in mourning? She imagined queuing in a shop somewhere. A woman, maybe that awful Mrs Quinn, behind her smelling the air, distinguishing the aroma from cheese smells, different tea leaves, buttermilk, soaps. The men serving with fresh cotton aprons. Maybe naphthalene faintly from herself. Mrs Quinn knowing the situation about her son. Sniffing the scents. Looking away from her. How dare she wear such stuff. Like a Jezebel. Her mouth tightening.

She was in for the night. By herself. She pushed up the sleeve of her cardigan and squeezed the atomiser bulb a couple of times. At first it gave little dry gasps. Then it exhaled extra coldness onto her bare wrist. As the perfume evaporated, it became cooler still. She raised her arm and turned her wrist upwards to smell it, took in the scent and closed her eyes. It was the best he could afford. He'd been at home a couple of Christmases ago and had been flush. And bought her this Chanel.

'For you, Mother, only the best.'

'I'll use it sparingly.'

This last time he'd been home he'd seemed on edge. When he was reading the paper, she'd catch him not moving his eyes, or staring up at the window in a kind of dwam as if unable to make sense of what he'd just read. She'd asked him what ailed him. In order to avoid the truth, he'd told her how he hated standing outlook when he was at sea. If it was rough, the regular whop of the bow into the waves. If the weather was better, the corrugated sea. At dawn the different bands of grey. Sea and sky, sometimes a horizon, sometimes no horizon. And when she asked him what he'd be looking out for, he hesitated. She worried away at him and, against his better judgement, he had said he'd be watching for any change that would indicate a submarine, or worse still a torpedo. An attack. A flick of white. Or if the sea was calm, the propeller sound of its approach. He told her of nights when nothing happened – all night long, seeing nothing but the dark Atlantic. The fear of falling asleep on his feet. Of letting everybody down. And before he knew where he was, he was talking to her about what he had been trying to *avoid* talking about. Voicing his fears to his mother. Baffling her with worry. And when he realised this, he backtracked. They were in convoys now for protection. 'Safety in numbers,' he said. 'That lengthens the odds a bit.' Evasive action could be taken. And nowadays destroyer escorts were routine – and they frightened most of the wolf packs away.

Not enough of them, it seemed. She'd got the news in a roundabout fashion. It was only a week since the doorbell rang. She was surprised because people usually just opened the door, came in and declared themselves.

She was making leftover soup at the time and the house was full of the smell of it. She'd answered the door and was surprised to see Father McBride. Her immediate thought was about the unwashed overall she was wearing. He raised his hat to her.

'Could I have a word?' he said. He was far too young to be a priest. Far too young to be wearing a hat.

She brought him into the sitting room and, when they were settled, he said that he just wanted to confirm something. He'd been talking to her son, Frank, the last time he was home. After Mass. In the course of the conversation Frank had happened to mention the name of the ship he was about to sail on – *Silverbirch*. Gracie confirmed it by nodding as if to say, yes, yes, that's the one. But she kept her mouth closed. Her insides were shaking. Ever since the *Athenia* had gone down on the first day of the war, only hours after war had been declared, she was uneasy. She'd been visiting a friend when the reports had come through on the wireless. Her friend shushed her and they both listened. The man kept saying the wrong word. He constantly talked about a German 'sumberine' and she knew that was not the right word. The German sumberine-this and the German sumberine-that. And the torpedoes. And all those people dead.

The priest cleared his throat, then produced a newspaper clipping from his pocket. Gracie said that her glasses were in the other room. She stood and her knees were like water. Father McBride followed her into the kitchen and extended his arm, offering her the clipping. She lifted her glasses from the mantelpiece and put them on, tilting the bit of paper to the window light. At first she was silent as she read – then she gasped and spoke out words that were not words at all, cries more like. The gist of the thing was that the *Silverbirch had been torpedoed and sunk 200 miles off the coast of Ireland. All twenty-five crew were missing, presumed dead.*

Father McBride said he was so sorry to be the bearer of such tidings. He was too shy a priest to hold onto her, too inexperienced to comfort her. He asked her if she knew anybody nearby she could call upon to be with her, and she was able to tell him about her niece, Letty, who lived just across the street. The priest went for her and, when he returned, Gracie was still in exactly the same position as when he had left. Letty, who by this time was crying herself, put her arms around her aunt and lowered her into the chair beside the fire. After a while Letty went into the kitchen and turned off the soup. Then offered to make tea. But the young priest looked flustered and opted out, saying he had a funeral to prepare for that evening. All he could think to do was to give a blessing to Gracie as she sat looking up at the light from the kitchen window.

Mumbling the text. Making the outlines of a cross with his right hand.

She remembered the words that had come out of her mouth earlier. 'Lost at sea is for ever.' Lacking a place to go, she had walked the dark house each night since she'd heard. At this time of year all her vases were empty. Sometimes she said things out loud in the different rooms but was unaware of what she was saying. 'Where have you gone, son? Where can I go to mourn you?' She had to keep a space for him inside her. Where he came from in the beginning. In place of a graveyard. He would be everywhere with her. And nowhere.

She went downstairs in time for the news at nine. Past her son's bicycle in the hall. Once she'd met him when she was coming back from the shops. He dismounted and walked beside her down the street – steering his bike from the back by simply holding the saddle. When they crossed a junction he bounced the front wheel up onto the pavement. She remarked on the deft way he had done it.

'My steed knows the way,' he said.

He loved westerns, that was another thing about him. He had told her once that horses had strange eyes – with horizontal pupils. Movies never showed that. Goats had them too, like black letter boxes. God knows where he got his information. When he was home on leave, or between jobs, he was never far away from the public library.

She switched on the wireless and sat down. It was habit. The only reason for listening had now gone. The worst had happened. Frank was lost. To be a grieving mother with no place to stand, no place to lay flowers. She could be knocked down and killed by a motor car and, the way she was feeling, that would be a blessing.

There was a distinct hiss on the Home Service and she adjusted the station by going past it, then back to it, with small twists until it was clearer. The talk was still about Mister Churchill. Always bloody Churchill. And about the bravery of the King and Queen. The voices on the BBC spoke about the dangers being faced by sailors and the valiant war they were fighting at sea. Too late for our Frank. Towards the end of the bulletin the talk was of the cold weather – its extremes.

She switched off. The fire was low but she couldn't be bothered doing anything about it. She sat staring down. Her mother and father had always talked about what they saw in the fire. They tried to make her see. 'Pictures of all sorts. There's a wee dog. On its hind legs.' Often they would resort to pointing with the tip of the poker. 'There – do you not see it?'

She heaved herself to her feet and went to the coalhouse in the yard. Her hand found the handle of the shovel. She knew the way, where to avoid the mangle, head high in the dark. The biggest mangle in the street. People had come looking to use it for eiderdowns, quilts, that kind of thing. She'd even made some friends out of it. When the handle was cranked, the rollers made a rumbling sound. It could even be adjusted for different thicknesses of material. Modern gadgets made things all so easy.

The fire sizzled when the coal was shovelled on. A mixture of smoke and steam rose into the chimney. She raked the ashes and tried to create a draught to introduce flame back into the grate. Then she stopped. She thought she'd heard the front door. She listened, not moving. The kitchen door opened almost immediately.

'It's only me.' Letty stood there, not knowing what to say. And visibly shaking.

It was cold. Bitterly so. Gracie put her head down, hiding as best she could beneath the felt hat she'd snatched from the hallstand on the way out. She tucked her chin into her scarf and made the best speed she could through the black streets and out onto the main road. Her toe caught on a flagstone and she nearly went down.

'Jesus.'

A couple of staggered steps righted her before she recovered her stride. There were trees on both sides of the road, and their roots had made mayhem of the pavements. Each foot she put out had to be an instant feeler. Between trees it was not so bad. She could increase her pace. It was like a night version of hopscotch. Then she heard a motor engine. She looked over her shoulder and watched a car come crawling past her. Its headlights had blackout covers so that the light could be faintly seen through the horizontal slits. Like horse pupils. Like goat eyes. But just enough illumination to see her own breath.

The car slowly pulled away, edging towards the Antrim Road until its sound was absorbed completely, leaving her listening to the sound of her own shoes on the pavement. It could snow, it was so cold. She was glad of her gloves.

Her mind was racing. Letty had talked of an early-evening performance. Would there be another one? Would the Capitol be closed? She couldn't believe, couldn't slow down her thoughts to examine them, to make any sense of what was happening. There was a shortcut down the steps to the park and along by Alexandra Gardens. The tippety motion of her feet descending at speed, then her stride lengthening as she passed the park railings. Left up the slope. Looking for the Capitol sign. Of course, fool that she was, the Capitol would have no lights on. Its sign had been doused. She was used to the sight of it before the war. Across the water some of the picture houses had closed when the war started, but they soon opened again because everyone created such a fuss. People needed romance. The bulk of the building sharpened as she approached it. She passed a hedge and saw that the car park was empty and her heart sank. She didn't turn on her heel, but went on in the hope that there might be some secretary there. Or cleaners. There was a complete absence of a plan in her head. She crossed the car park. In the wide-open space it was beginning to freeze. There was a crisp sound to her footsteps but she did not look down. Her eyes were on the building looming above her. It still looked new and fresh – that creamy colour – with modern rounded corners. It had a canopy over its front double doors and she saw a movement. Like an animal's eyes. Aware of movement, before she knew what had caused the movement. It was a man. In his overcoat, stepping outside the cinema doors and stooping to lock them. She gasped aloud – then called.

'Excuse me.'

He stopped what he was doing and switched on a torch and shone it on her face. Seeing a woman, he lowered the beam.

'Can I help you?'

'I was hoping there'd be another showing.'

'I'm sorry, Missus – the place is closed.' His voice sounded matter-of-fact. He switched off the torch and slid it into his raincoat pocket. 'As you can see, I'm locking up. That's it for the night.'

She didn't know what to say. The man was wearing a navy raincoat and hat. She turned on her heel and began to retrace her steps through the car park. Walking slowly because she didn't know what to do. The man standing on the veranda looked after her. He spoke aloud.

'If you're really keen, there's an afternoon show tomorrow. Starts at half two.'

This made her turn. She stood watching him, her arms straight by her sides. The man shrugged and lifted his hat to her.

'Goodnight.'

She put her hands in her pockets and walked deliberately towards him. He seemed a little unnerved by this, as if she was going to produce a weapon of some sort.

'It's a great picture, right enough,' he said. 'You can always rely on Cary Grant.'

'It wasn't the big picture I wanted to see. It was the News.'

'Why – what was on?'

Gracie could not find the words to explain. The porch was terrazzo and the sound of her shoes became louder as she stepped up.

'It's been a long day,' said the man. He pocketed his keys, readjusted the fedora on his head and moved to step down from the veranda. Gracie remained where she was.

She began to weep, or to make the noises of weeping. The man took out his torch again and shone it in her face. There were definitely tears.

'Are you all right?' he said.

Not trusting her voice, she shook her head from side to side vigorously. No, I am not all right. The man switched off and pocketed the torch. He reached out and touched her sleeve.

She began to shake. He steadied her, holding her arm firmly through her coat. Again he said, 'Are you sure you're okay?'

The man stood looking at her, wondering.

'Maybe we should get you inside,' he said, almost to himself. He took out his keys again and unlocked the glass doors.

'I'm far from all right,' said Gracie. 'But I'm not mad in the head.'

'Glad to hear it. What's wrong?'

Again she shook her head, unable to explain.

The man sighed.

'Come in and sit down for a minute,' he said. He led her into the porch, held the inner doors open for her. 'Over here – this way.' He shone the torch at her feet crossing the plush red carpet – as if he was an usherette. 'In here.' He unlocked the office door and switched on the light. She saw he was about the same age as herself. Late forties or fifty. He took off his hat and dropped it on the desk. Gracie noticed that he glanced up at the wall to see the time. It was just after half past ten. How awful to be keeping this man out of his bed. She seemed reluctant to sit down. But he insisted.

'I'm sorry,' she said. She discovered her handkerchief in her pocket and tried to clean up her face. 'I'm so sorry.' Then she took off her gloves and stuffed them into her pockets.

'Is there anyone I can contact for you?' There was a telephone on the desk.

'No,' she said. 'You're very kind.'

He hesitated. Then moved round the desk and sat down.

'I'm Johnny – the manager here. Johnny Canavan. Always the last man out.' He smiled. 'What are we going to do with you?'

'I'm in a bit of a state, right enough.'

'We get all sorts here. Guys singing. Going round with the cap. Probably make as much as me. They can't afford an instrument, so they do Bing Crosby or Nelson Eddy – maybe both at the same time.'

He laughed at his own joke. She blew her nose again and looked up at him. 'I'm Gracie. From Baltic Avenue.'

'Gracie who?'

'O'Brien.' She said, 'I don't know where to start.'

'At the beginning.'

There was a long silence. She made several intakes of breath before she spoke.

'I lost my son – Frank – a week ago. At sea. His ship was torpedoed. In mid-Atlantic.'

'I'm so sorry to hear that.'

'And because . . . I like to go to the pictures with my niece . . . Letty's her name. But given the circumstances . . . I didn't want to come out tonight.'

'I understand.'

'She always falls asleep when the warm air hits her. She went with a friend tonight. Anne. And Anne wakens Letty

16

up in the middle of the Pathé News. She said she was still half asleep, but she saw them landing people at Galway. And she thought one of them was him. But she says she couldn't be sure. The man was in no fit state . . . '

'Yes, I've seen that newsreel this week. What age is your niece?'

'A grown woman – mother of two and another one on the way.'

'So she's no whippersnapper.'

'She says she thought it was our Frank.' Gracie said, 'But she says it was only the slightest glimpse. And she only saw it once.'

Johnny raised his eyebrows and looked at her.

'The friend she was with – did she get a look . . . ?'

'Anne? She doesn't even know our Frank. Never met him.'

Johnny pulled a face. She could see he was trying to work out if she was out of her mind. It was something to do with the length of the pauses she was taking. Trying to size her up. And why not? She had landed on his doorstep in tears in the middle of the night with a garbled story. Grief could do this to people.

'I want to see for myself,' said Gracie. 'Would that be a terrible thing to ask? I don't know what it involves.'

'My projectionist is away home.'

Gracie put her head in her hands and stayed like that for some time.

'Where does he live?' she said without looking up.

'I don't even know if he'd be at home. Hughie likes a drink after work.'

Gracie leaned back in her chair and looked into the air to stop herself crying again.

'Is there *any* way I could see it?'

Johnny smiled and shook his head. He looked again at the clock.

'I'm not much of a projectionist,' he said. 'I *used* to know how. Been a long time.' He stood. 'But you don't forget – like riding a bicycle. Only thing is you can tear the film. In the machine, if you haven't the knack. They don't like you doing that. Films get shorter, the older they are.'

'Sorry.'

'The more they're shown, the more damaged they get. It chews them up.'

He went to a wooden cupboard on the wall by the door and selected a bunch of keys.

'Would you like to follow me?'

She rose and walked to the door. Her fists were clenched, her pockets full of gloves. Johnny stood with his hand on the light switch. When the light went out, she stood still in the dark lobby. The torch clicked on and its circle of light around her feet led her to the staircase. Their enlarged shadows moved on the stuccoed walls.

'Do you mind if I call you Gracie?'

'It's my name.'

He switched on the staircase lights. She so loved this carpet and its wooden banisters, its opulence. The only sound was the padding of their feet in the deep pile of the carpet.

'It might take a bit of time to set up,' Johnny said. 'I don't want to leave you on your own. So – ' he indicated a direction with his hand. Upstairs, they walked a corridor of the same carpet. The walls were covered with framed posters for previous films.

They came to a black door, which Johnny opened with his bunch of keys. The carpet ended beyond the door and the flooring was just concrete. He went through a second door and switched on a light. A dim bulb hung from the ceiling.

'This is where all the magic happens,' he said. The room was small and full to the ceiling with black projectors – difficult, in the gloom, for Gracie to tell how many. There were wheels and spools at head height.

'Like mangles,' she said.

Johnny smiled at her description as he rummaged through large circular tins. He was talking to himself or reading labels. There wasn't much room and Johnny had to excuse himself as he eased past her. She pressed herself back into the wall. He sniffed the air.

'Hughie must have got his hands on some nifty soap.'

'Lavender?' she said.

'How would I know?'

'It might be me.' She pulled an apologetic face. 'I didn't know I was going out.'

Johnny paused and looked at her.

'I'm not sure what's . . . '

'Never mind,' she said. 'I should button my lip.' She folded her arms while he continued to look through the aluminium tins.

'This is going to take a bit of time,' he said. 'Maybe you should have a seat.' She looked around but there wasn't a seat of any kind. Not even a stool.

'I'm okay.'

'I can't find what I'm looking for. Hughie has his own system.'

'Maybe it doesn't matter.'

'Oh, it does. It does. Now that I know what it's about.'

'You're far too good. Will somebody be expecting you?'

'Not at all,' he said with a shake of his head. 'Let me show you to a seat. I can never make any headway when somebody's watching me. I'll put a light on down below.' He checked that he had used the right switch by looking through the small window into the hall of the cinema. Then he led Gracie out of the projection room, along to the doors into the balcony.

'Sit at the front,' he said. 'Best seats in the house.' He turned and went back along the corridor. Gracie went gingerly down the stairs in semi-darkness towards the screen, stepping sideways. The only light was from the screen area. The curtains were closed, heavy brocade, the same red colour as the carpets. They hung in measured columns from a pelmet of the same material. The air smelled of stale cigarette smoke – some disinfectant, but different from the Lyceum.

The place was silent. She had never been in a picture house when it was like this. Normally between showings, after the curtains had swished across and the lights had come on, there were conversations – talk that rose to such an extent you had to shout to be heard, or cup your ear to listen to what was being said. Everybody was talking about what they thought of the film – the bits they liked, what frightened them most. People took the opportunity to go to the toilets. Those who had no need stood to let others past, and the noise of seats springing up could be heard all over the place. But now you could hear the slightest thing. The sound of her own clothing, a squeak of a door from the projection box. A distant clatter. A single cough.

She sat down in the front row. The only times she'd been up here before were for some treat or other. Movies were the same, whether viewed from stalls or balcony. But to be up here was an added extra. Greater knee room. The vault above her, the rake of the seats so steep no one could block her view – no matter what kind of a hat they were wearing. The ashtrays for the front seats were screwed to the balustrade and were filled to overflowing. Some job for the cleaners in the morning. The only picture she remembered seeing from up here was *The Good Earth* with Paul Muni and Luise Rainer. That was a love picture and a half. Luise Rainer acted a poverty-stricken Chinawoman. The whole of China was at war – in chaos. And your woman finds a wee bag of jewellery in the street and hides it in her dress. Enough to support her family for the rest of her life. But then she's arrested and the firing squad is executing looters. There and then. And you actually see that – people being shot and killed. But before she can be searched, the firing squad is ordered to move on. And, thanks be to God, your woman is spared.

It was enough to put the heart sideways in her, then as now. Being in the balcony felt like she was in the lower jaw of some huge beast about to swallow her. She kept looking up over her shoulder to check the small square of the projectionist's window. The beam that came from there on ordinary nights was luminous with cigarette smoke. The images it carried to the screen could be seen writhing within its corridor of light.

Poor Letty – she was so good. Standing on the threshold of Gracie's living room, she'd started to cry. Gracie tried to coax whatever it was out of her. Then, when she *did* tell her what she thought she'd seen, her aunt was flustered and upset, found it difficult to swallow. 'How in the name of God . . . ?' The girl was half dreaming, maybe. Exhausted from looking after her children from morning till night. Not to mention being pregnant. Letty hadn't been sure, telling her story. She'd just been resting her eyes, she said. Her friend Anne had elbowed her back to life. And it was then that she'd seen what she *thought* she saw. Letty had asked her aunt if she wanted to go to the cinema to see for herself. No, Gracie had said, there wouldn't be another showing. It was too late. Letty offered to go back with her. To hold her hand, as it were. To simply ask. It wouldn't take her a minute to run across the road and tell Tommy she'd be another wee while – I mean, given the circumstances. Tommy was so easy-going. But Gracie had insisted she would catch one of the programmes tomorrow and see for herself. 'It'll be absolutely nothing,' she said. 'You go home to your man and your wains and never think another thing about it.' And Letty had kissed her on the forehead and urged her to try and get some sleep. But at the very word 'sleep', Gracie knew it would never come to her unless she made certain, unless she checked. When the sound of Letty closing the front door had ceased to echo in the hallway, Gracie was on her feet walking towards the hallstand for her coat.

The curtains parted from the middle, then stopped with a clunking noise. She looked round. Johnny was making a mess of things, God love him. But she so wished he wouldn't.

'Oh, come on, come on,' she said. Her stomach was in knots. The curtain mechanism whirred into life again and the curtains swished slowly open, baring the blank screen. It looked grey. She sat forward in her seat. There was what seemed like an interminable wait for the flickering images to begin. At first numbers came – in descending order. Then the newsreel's logo leapt onto the screen. The flapping white rooster. It crowed at the same time as the brassy soundtrack. The sound was different when there was no one else in the cinema. Hollow. Echoing. But very loud.

The posh newsreel voice spoke at great speed to get the most words in. One moment full of sneer, the next full of would-you-believe-it condescension. The pictures were of royalty and palaces. Out and about, visiting their distressed population. The voice talked about the King and how good and generous he was. Shaking hands with the unwashed, when there was no need to shake hands. It talked about the Queen and how good and generous she was to be with him. Horses prancing up or down the Mall in front of open carriages. Feathers blowing in their headgear. Constant toe-tapping music.

And then the newsreel voice switches to an item about the Battle of the Atlantic. At the very word 'Atlantic' she feels her stomach plummet. Ships, from horizon to horizon, sailing through the moonlit darkness in formation. Then, in close-up, one of them is ruptured by an explosion. Black smoke billows up. Gracie admits out loud that she cannot watch. But neither can she look away. And still the newsreader's voiceover goes on and on. He talks of survivors.

About landing them at Galway in neutral Ireland. But there is no indication of which ship it is. A nameless hull towers above a dock. A gangplank diagonal on the screen. Two solemn men carry a stretcher down its slope onto dry land. The man on the stretcher turns his face to the camera. But it is an old face, one Gracie has never seen in her life. And then two girls, both smiling, come walking down, holding onto each other. The patronising cheerful voiceover, 'If any more German submarines are knocking around, they'd better watch out. These ladies mean business.' Two men with blankets over their shoulders, both in stockinged feet, stare. Neither is Frank. Garda officers, with hats too large for them, reach out to help. Gracie daren't take her eyes off the screen. She thinks she has not blinked since the newsreel began. Then to the left of the screen, in a huddle of blanketed men, there he is. Our Frank. Jesus Christ, the night. A blanket over his head, his hair stuck to his face. He has survived. Before he turns away he even manages a smile for the cameraman and, with the wonders of film, it is also a smile for her, his mother. And I thought you were dead. Within a second her elation changes to concern. He's hurt – burned, by the look of it. The galloping newsreel voice says something about the flaming sea left behind by ships that sink. Infernos afloat. She can see the hurt in her son's face, his staring and shadowed eyes. And then the camera is away. Somewhere else. About football. A crowd of thousands. One team in white. The voice going on about something that doesn't concern her. Then the concluding music, and again the white rooster crowing fit to burst. The image disappears.

Silence.

The double doors in the balcony are edged with felt. She hears them open quietly and brush closed. Johnny comes down the steps to her. She begins to wail. She says, 'It's him. It's our Frank. He's alive.'

Johnny sits, puts his hand on her shoulder and pats her overcoat to help stop her crying. He says her name over and over again.

'Gracie, Gracie, Gracie . . . '

Outside the cinema Johnny locked up. Gracie stood waiting. The sky had partially cleared and a moon had become visible. They walked together through the car park. The frost had intensified and crisped beneath their feet. Gracie almost slipped, her arms shot up to keep balance.

'All right?' said Johnny.

'Steady as she goes.'

Johnny kept looking at her and she was aware of being looked at.

'I dunno what to say,' she said.

'I'm not surprised. It's not every day such things happen.'

They came to the crossroads and stopped. Johnny's hand edged to his hat to bid her farewell.

'I can't thank you enough,' she said. 'You've been so kind.'

He shook his head as if it was nothing.

'It's very dark,' he said. 'I'll walk you down home.' He steered her towards Baltic Avenue, his hand nudging her elbow for a moment.

'There's no need.'

But she knew there was. They touched shoulders now and again as they negotiated the icy pavement.

'I'll have to tell Letty. If she's still up.'

'Waken her.' Johnny was grinning. She could hear the grin in his voice. 'Hey, Gracie, that was some newsreel.'

She agreed, nodding her head, afraid she'd start weeping again. They both heard their own footsteps.

'One more thing you can help me with, Mister Canavan.'

He turned up his palm to the moonlight as if to say – anything at all.

'Tell me how to get to Galway tomorrow?'

GLASSHOUSES

The old man leaned on the iron guardrail, looking down into the water. His weight was on his elbows and he was looking to see some movement in the depths. His two grandchildren had climbed up onto a ledge to be in a position to see beneath the green water weed that almost covered the surface of the indoor pond. The older of the two was Dan, a boy of nine. His sister Mina was five. She was on her first holiday from school. Being the grandfather, he was looking after them. It was quiet in the glasshouse, but some other children's voices could be heard from a distance.

He knew from his many walks in this place that there were bigger, darker fish to be seen. There was a constant sound of water feeding in and draining out. The surface weed was always on the move – something was disturbing it from underneath. The movement would slowly create a gap and then close over again – little swirls and ruffles moved about. Beneath the surface the water was dark, almost black, except where there were some pale-grey pipes. Probably for warming the water, kidding the fish they lived and swam in foreign climes. The grandfather was trying to catch sight of one of the big fish to point it out to Dan. Long ago he'd figured out the big ones were catfish of some sort. If the boy got excited by spricks, he'd go daft about the big ones. Now the water went still and became a mirror. He saw his reflection – and the struts of the clear glass roof above him. He looked up to check. The panes were flexing in the storm.

Behind them there were small square tanks full of weed. Bubbles rose to the surface through the dense underwater greenery. Mina had to be lifted up to see the many tiny fish zigzagging about in there.

'They're the grandchildren of the big ones in the pond.'

Seeing them side-on, they were little snippets of colour – rainbow flecks dodging in and out the strings of weed. Hundreds of them.

'If kingfishers were fish, that's what they'd look like.'

He set Mina down on the ground. She did not let go of his hand. It was like holding a wee prawn. Her hands were always cold.

'You can let go now,' he said. She took her hand away and let it hang by her side.

And then he saw it.

'Dan. Mina.' He pointed into the water. He wanted to give the boy a fright. 'A big brute of a thing.' A black fish drew its length across the diagonal of an underwater pipe. 'Look at the barbels round its mouth.'

'Where?' Dan wasn't quick enough to see and the weed closed over again.

'Keep looking,' said the grandfather.

'Let me see,' said Mina, long after the fish had gone.

'I never seen it,' said the boy.

'You will, you will some day.' The old man settled onto his elbows again, his eyes watching the floating lettuce-coloured weed as a clue to what was beneath. Trying to assess its size – Moby-Dick or sprick? He went on talking to the boy, 'Barbels are to fish what whiskers are to a cat. In the dark they can feel their way.'

But when he looked to see what Dan thought, the boy was no longer there. Nor was Mina. So much for information. He'd scared them off again. And then of course the weed opened, the pale pipe appeared and the carp-like fish cruised its slow length back over it again, every detail clear. Always the way.

This indoor pond was at the top of a passageway, like the eye of a needle – more of a horseshoe. It was part of the route he liked to walk on his own, looking here and there, watching out for the different flowers and plants that bloomed throughout the year. No walk was ever the same. If there was a sameness, it was in his constant bending over to smell the new plants that had blossomed since his last visit.

The three of them had come in the back gate of the park – all the quicker to avoid the bad weather. The rain blowing and the wind whirling up the fallen leaves. Such storms were becoming the norm. Each winter that passed was proving the science – forest fires and melting glaciers. Except for presidents and dunderheads.

Coming in the back gate meant they were walking widdershins through the two glasshouses. One was more modern, with different sections of the world and its climates. The other – now the furthest away – a white Victorian-domed extravaganza. Icing sugar and isinglass.

He was continually explaining and pointing out things to the children. Mina just listened, and when her grandfather looked at her or addressed anything directly to her, she bit her lip and smiled. The boy always answered with questions. 'Who lives here? Does anybody live here when we go home? Are people buried in here?' It was in his nature. At home when he was visiting he'd say with his serious face, 'Granda, are you really the oldest man in Scotland? Granda, when are you going to die? Why do you wear the same clothes every day?'

He joined his hands behind his back and set off in the direction the children had gone. He would stop and be amazed at things he hadn't seen before, despite having walked this route hundreds of times. He read a new label for something called 'Soursop, prickly Custard-Apple'. The kids would like that. He'd have to find them and tell them. Old man's beard he knew and loved. Beside it was a plant of blue-and-red spires he had never seen before. He leaned forward and sought the label at root level. 'Blue Rain,' it said. How amazing. He walked on out of the doorway, out of the horseshoe section. As always, he turned left and looked down the aisle. The kids must have run ahead.

At home he had a mantelpiece – his museum, he called it – full of things found, things he had bought, objects he had noticed or thought unusual. A delicate bird skull he'd found in a sand dune, a filigree of bones from a fish tail lifted from a pier. Fossils he'd bought on holiday, halved and polished ammonites. Geodes that were cracked in two, and he had joined them so that the join was a secret, something not noticed. He'd hold the two halves of the plain stone together in front of the grandchild's face, then open them like a hinged box and reveal the jewellery within, the purple amethyst sparkle. Always a winner. A stone transformed. From a simple rock to a brooch. Stones not to be thrown in any glasshouse, he chuckled.

A couple came into the long aisle. As they approached, he smelled a commercial perfume that overpowered any smell the plants gave off. The couple were not speaking. Of course the perfume could be from the man. Aftershave. Old Spice or some such. He had never felt the need of it. He held his breath until the couple were well past. Where were those wains? They must have moved on into the next section, the one he knew contained the banana tree. 'Can you eat those bananas?' would be Dan's next question. 'Would they poison you?' But when he got there, there was no one. He stopped at a new hanging flower as elegant as two sides of a zip and read its label. The botanists who ran the place supplied information on laminated cards. He loved the way they were written. Both outside and in the glasshouses the trees were labelled, hung with little stories. The wood of a holly tree was used for making chessmen – also the hammers of harpsichords and the butts of billiard cues. In medieval Ireland it was used for chariot shafts. Holly wood? They were making movies now in Ireland as good as anything he'd seen as a boy.

And there were plaques on park benches. He thought them better than any gravestones. 'For Lily and George, who loved to sit here.' Another one had sunrise and sunset dates, in place of birth and death years. Instead of a plaque, a bench was engraved with the words 'We're all on a speck in space for a tick in time.'

In the same vein inside the second glasshouse, he liked what they had to say about 'The Wollemi pine', a species of tree from 200 million years ago, which was thought to have become extinct two million years ago. Until some tree guy on an Australian walking holiday found specimens just outside Sydney in 1994. The botanical find of the century. Recently it had been in the news about the Australian bush fires. The firefighters attempting to protect the last Wollemi pines anywhere on the planet. Trees that used to cover the whole of Australia. The word 'wollemi' was Aboriginal and meant 'look around you, keep your eyes open and watch out'.

He tore himself away, decided he'd better hurry, keep his eyes open and catch up with the grandchildren. The next place was the jungle, the highest room, the hottest air, with tall trees stooping where they met the glass roof. Tarzan vines hung down. The place was being watered but he couldn't see who was doing it. Water clattered down from a hose onto the broad leaves and splashed onto the grid floor at the crossroads in the jungle. There were leaves that looked like they had grown on backwards. Leaves that looked upside-down. Some of the leaves were huge – big enough to wrap children.

The door into the next place – the desert – needed some oil and it screeched when he pulled it. The zone was empty and the fall in temperature noticeable. One time before, he had been in this place with Dan and the boy had asked about the spines on the cacti. 'Would they kill you if you touched them?' He'd allowed the boy to touch a single spine with the tip of his finger. 'Very gently,' he

warned. 'I don't want to see any blood.' The child had
ouched and pantomimed and sucked his finger. 'Enough.
Enough,' said his grandfather. Now, as he hurried through,
he saw again the boy's face, the feigned astonishment, the
play-acting.

Where on earth were those children? It was doing
nothing for his blood pressure. At the very thought, he
felt a pain in his chest. Not a pain, a discomfort of sorts.
And then he remembered the day before, for quite some
time during the afternoon he'd had a pain in his upper
arm. He was old enough to know that this was not a pain
in his upper arm, it was known as 'referred pain' and
stemmed from his heart.

Into the flower house, the last place they could be.
There was another horseshoe extension, architecturally to
balance the first. The flowers filled the place with a fra-
grance. He always found it difficult in here to trace the
origin of individual aromas. Which flower was giving off
which smell. So that he had eventually to bend down and
bring his nose close, to identify which smell belonged to
which bloom. But not today. He dashed around the
horseshoe and, because there was nobody there, he called
out for the first time. He did not want to appear foolish.
'Dan.' But there was no answer. 'Mina.' The floor tiles
squidged beneath his feet as he accelerated to the exit door
of the glasshouse.

Some Japanese tourists with cameras were coming in.
He stepped back and smiled, ushered them in. There were
two elderly women in the party and they had stopped
outside to talk. He held the door open for them, trying
to entice them in more quickly. They smiled their thanks

to him and he stepped out into the weather. The rain had stopped but the wind was still there – ruffling the lying water, darkening it. The sky seemed concave, pressing down on him. A Vitamin D-free zone. He looked all around. There were a few people about, moving mostly from one glasshouse to the other for shelter. But no children. The boy, Dan, already knew about the white-domed Victorian building, knew it would be next on the route of their journey. Maybe he would have anticipated it – knowing the regularity of his grandfather's routine. And gone ahead with his wee sister. Christ, he had to check it out.

It was now beginning to look serious. But he had to try. Where in the world had they got to? To be away from the first glasshouse for as little time as possible, just in case they should still be there, he half ran, half walked to the doors of the Victorian glasshouse. It had a fishpond in the entrance area. Dan might have remembered that. There were some children peering through the railings down into the water. The fish were smears of orange. Some with white markings, some with black. They moved around beneath the surface. The water was surprisingly opaque, he couldn't see to any real depth. None of the children looked anything like Dan or Mina. But he had no time for the languid fish. He headed for the central section. This was circular, the place beneath the glass dome. Palm trees, craggy bushes, some blooming, some not, a tree with leaves as smooth as silk, again the sound of running water. He ran, looking always over his shoulder into the centre. There was definitely a discomfort now in the middle of his chest – like wind. As if a ball was sitting there, slowly expanding. Or a belt around his upper body had tightened a notch. He stopped running and tried to burp. But he couldn't get under it to get it shifted. He kept on walking. And swallowing. If only he could . . . He belched and immediately felt the situation improve. The rain must have started up again, and the gale was buffeting the dome above. Sounded like hail rattling against the glass. He felt the need to call out names again, in case they were hiding in the bushes of the centre space. 'Dan. Mina.' A flat kind of a sound spiralling up into the dome. Would they hear that? If they were here? Would his calling be drowned by the storm?

Last year he had watched a series on TV called *Reported Missing*. The documentaries were made from recorded fragments – the first phone call to the emergency services, interviews with the distraught family, comments by the forensic experts, the thoughts of concerned policemen or policewomen – until the search was finally resolved, should it be overnight or five years, should it be mischief or murder. A good advert for the cops. Here were men and women in uniform being kind. Presenting a different face from the normal TV deviousness. Brutality. Bullying. But how could he even think of such a thing? Calling the police. The children were missing for about five minutes. Boo! They would pop out of the next bush to give him a fright. 'Sorry, Officer, found them. You can call off the squad cars.' Nee-naw. Nee-naw in the background. He had now completed the circuit and had not seen them. Jesus.

What would his daughter say? How could he tell her? He just knew, watching her playing with them, how much

she cherished them. But it was too soon. He was catas-
trophising, as usual. He tried to stop. To think of something
different. Beside the entrance were two rooms – one was
for photographing weddings, the other housed all sorts of
carnivorous plants. He disliked the tabloid way they tried
to entice people, especially children, into this domain.
Posters for pitcher plants, Venus flytraps, bladderwort.
School drawings of spiders and cartoons of flies screaming.
The right-wing press pandering to the worst in us. Drama
in acquiring protein. He stepped inside and looked around
the door. An old woman was the only one there, gazing
down at a patch of sundews. He closed the door and headed
for the exit, but continued to think of the pitcher plants,
their wiles, the way they enticed. He thought of his two
grandchildren meeting some man. Not a tramp, but
somebody ordinary who looked at them through half-
closed eyes. Offering to answer Dan's questions. Maybe
giving Mina a sweet. Taking her by the hand. The children
were both utterly naive. They were used to good people
around them. They would assume that everybody was good.
Dan would be on his best behaviour. 'We've lost our granda.'
Or would he say, 'We've become separated from our grandfather. Can you please help?' Because he'd been taught by
his parents to be polite. And the strange man would say, 'I
will bring you to your grandfather. Follow me.'

Again he was making a catastrophe out of it. The River
Kelvin was not far away, hidden in undergrowth, down
a set of new, darkly tarmacked steps. Out of sight, away
from passers-by. He felt it was difficult to breathe, his
heart was racing. He must calm down. He stopped and

breathed in slowly. Stood still. Spicy, odd smells, like tea, cinnamon, rosemary, musk. In a corner in front of him there were little whirlwinds of flies – small as dust motes – endlessly dodging each other.

Fifty years ago he would have prayed – but those days were long gone. He took a fit of coughing and, when it had stilled, he moved on. Through the exit, outside into the storm again. Because now that he had checked they were not in the Victorian house, he must return to the first glasshouse and search for them there. Where he had last seen them. Did a phrase like 'last seen them' mean the same as 'seen them for the last time'? He half ran, half walked, his head down into the rain, back to the first glasshouse. He powered through the place of blooms and scents, around its first horseshoe, edging past people, saying, 'Excuse me' far too often. Through the desert region with its no hiding place, with its cacti and succulents bristling with spikes. Into the high-ceilinged jungle house, still dripping with water, where he caught up with the two Japanese grandmothers staring up at the Tarzan vines. But no grandchildren. Into the banana place, with its single bunch of green bananas on show. Past the corridor of high, dark greens that had grown itself into a tunnel. To the begonia house, where it had all begun among the dished leaves, the speckled ones, ones that looked like they'd been in a room when you were whitewashing the ceiling and they'd got splattered, octagonal ones, ones composed of blue and green fur, ones with pink-petalled flowers, like flowers in disguise. And there, by the furthest-away door to the fishpond where he last saw them, stood his two grandchildren. Like Hansel and Gretel. 'Thanks be to Jesus and his holy mother.'

They must have turned right instead of left.

'Hi,' he said.

'Hi,' said both the children.

Smiles all round.

'Where did you two get to?'

'We went back in to see the fish again,' said Dan.

'Ten minutes ago?' He managed to keep his voice calm. 'I wondered where you'd gone.'

Subtly shifting the blame onto them. But now he was in good form. He put his hands on their heads, ruffled their hair. Made jokes they did not understand. Sang little snatches of old songs. He wondered if there were rich cities on the equator that had glasshouses with zones in them to represent Scotland under its lid of grey – with wet and windy rooms, places of damp and cold, where people could step out of the glasshouse into a world of heat and sunlight. He belched loudly and the children laughed and pointed at him. That was a joke they understood. The wee girl even finger-wagged him. But his chest eased – loosened several notches. And he knew he would make light of the whole thing to his daughter, tell her it was as if he'd been searching throughout the world, the deserts and the oceans and the waterways, the jungles and mountains, high up and low down, for something he'd already held in the palm of his hand.

SOUP MIX

It was meant to be an all-day meeting. One of those things at the last minute where he had to be there, face-to-face. Even Skype wouldn't do. And he cursed his boss from the moment he got up in the dark. Also in the taxi, ploughing through the rain to the airport. It was a meeting about strategy and could have been easily conducted by email. But for the boss it was a power thing, and he wanted to see him on the other side of the desk. He lolled and swung in his chair – his body language said I'm in charge – he wore no tie and his top shirt button was undone. Out came his favourite phrases, 'The way I see it' and 'To be honest with you'. The reason he wanted him over was to make sure 'we are on the same page'. It turned out that it was the boss who had to call things to a halt because he had another unexpected, but urgent, lunch meeting on the other side of the city.

And there he was 'standing idly by' on the street corner of his own home town, with the strap of his shoulder bag cutting into him. He knew if he submitted travel expenses there would be questions asked about the extra taxi, so he decided to use public transport. It had been so long since he had taken a bus here that he had to ask an inspector – to be told the new number and the stop to get on.

He went upstairs for the view. It was almost empty. His anger and resentment at the boss began to recede and he relaxed. He now had more than enough time before his return flight. He sat in the front seat and, because it made him feel like a boy again, he put one foot up on the ledge below the window. The journey was familiar because this was where his mother had lived. He knew the parks, each church spire they passed – and there were many of them – the wooded suburbs, the olive-green mountain in the distance. It was spring, coming up to Easter. Because he was on the top deck he seemed on a level with the trees, almost *in* the trees. He could see green buds sprouting, cherry trees becoming pink. Putting forth blossom. He didn't often think like this, in this poetic way. But the meeting ending early had put him in a good mood. The sun was out, heightening everything.

He got off at the correct stop and crossed the main road. There was a row of shops, and a group of schoolgirls in the dark-green uniform of the local Catholic school were queuing outside a fish-and-chip shop. The girls all tried to individualise what they were wearing – a striped tie pulled into a tight knot, shirts unbuttoned at the neck, white socks pushed down to exactly the same length. And corrugated in exactly the same way. Most of them had their shoelaces tucked down the sides of their shoes, rather than tied. The girls were loud – squealing and clowning, their speech full of swearing and bad language.

'Showing off,' his mother would have called it. 'Drawing attention to themselves.'

Slightly apart from the queue was a group of Muslim girls, who wore the hijab and had long skirts in school colours that reached the pavement. His mother would have approved. Her style mantra was to wear clothes 'high to the neck and low to the ankles'. Not so much to his mother's taste were a few of the Muslim girls who wore bright and colourful headgear, which looked a little like the Sydney Opera House. They're going to school, not a fashion parade, his mother would have said.

The greengrocer's produce was on display outside his shop. There were bouquets of flowers already made up, wrapped in cellophane. He chose one of carnations, in the middle price range, and brought it into the shop.

'I'll take these.'

'Lovely day,' said the greengrocer. He was portly and bald, had obviously been in the trade all his life. He was dressed in a navy apron with the franchise logo on its bib.

There was a bucket beside his feet with some more spring flowers in it. The greengrocer nodded down to them.

'These are reduced – a wee bit past their best, but they'd make a nice display.' He waited for his customer to say something.

'How long will they last?'

'More than a day or two,' he said. 'Half price?'

'Okay.' The man plucked a bunch from the bucket and set them on the counter.

'Good decision.'

Water splashed from the stems onto the counter. The assistant began to wrap both bunches in the same slice of brown paper.

The noise of traffic diminished, the further he walked from the main road. Processions of the schoolgirls had gone off down a different road, most of them eating from white polystyrene. It became quiet enough for him to hear the noise of the cellophane and brown paper brushing against his leg as he walked.

The whole suburb was like one large garden. It seemed to have a microclimate of its own, which led to the cherry blossom being further advanced and the trees more densely covered. Blackbirds were singing and a dog startled him when it began to bark close by. When he drew level, he saw it was an Alsatian and was glad to see a gate between him and it. The gate vibrated with the onslaught of barking and pawing. He stepped away, walked close to the kerb. The dog followed him along inside the garden hedge, still barking. It was the same kind of feeling he got when there were wasps about. He turned into the long, straight avenue where the Home was.

His mother would get a bit of a surprise. She wasn't expecting him, because he hadn't phoned to say he would be in town. Not that it would make much difference. Normally he would phone and alert the staff to his visit. And they would tell her and keep reminding her. But her memory was going. In conversation, she would repeat herself many times. Whatever was currently in her head. Again and again. The same repetition of a story, nose-to-tail. On his last visit she'd been on about the time he'd been seriously ill. He was about eight, at the time. The doctor had said there was little could be done. She always told him about the aunt who was so concerned she checked that his breathing could fog the mirror of her powder compact.

'We didn't know whether you were going to live or die. I sat up at your bedside for three days and three nights – just dozing in the armchair – until you came round, until you were more like yourself.'

When she first went into the Home a year ago his reaction was to say, 'Yes, you've just told me that.' But it made no difference. She told him again. The best thing to do was to nod and smile and change the subject.

'Is that a blackbird or a thrush?' And his mother would turn and look down into the garden.

'Where?'

He saw movement down by the gates of the Home. A nurse whose coat didn't quite cover the white of her uniform walked to the middle of the road and waved people across. Like a lollipop lady. A line crossing from pavement to pavement. At the back of the line was another nurse. The small procession came towards him. From a distance they looked like schoolchildren. But they didn't sound like it. They were silent. Both men and women. Grey and white hair, shuffling gait, bald heads. Some of the women were in pairs, linked arm-in-arm. One or two had a stick or a cane. Then he saw his mother in the middle of them, walking alone.

He was unsure what to do. Should he cross the road and greet her? He'd have to halt the procession. Stoop to kiss her, in front of all the others? Any time he'd visited her in the Home before, there'd been such a clucking and fussing from everyone. It would be embarrassing. Would he have to get permission from the nurse? To talk to his mother? The way you would if it was a line of infants? His mother would become so flustered. Or maybe she wouldn't recognise him – maybe she had deteriorated since his last visit. What would he do if she looked up at him and said, 'Who are you?'

It was so typical that she was walking on her own. She could be perfectly friendly, but there were other times when she could be very aloof. She'd said to him, 'I have very little in common with the ones in here. They're not my style. Yet I do everything I can for them.'

All of his life he'd thought of her as a stylish dresser. On school sports days she stood out amongst the other parents. She wore navy suits, high heels, a stylish hat – whether the day demanded it or not. A pillbox rakishly tilted. Sometimes even a fascinator. Did she think she was at a wedding?

'Everything must match,' she would say. 'Otherwise, what's the point?' There were times she even tried to match the colour of her wristwatch strap to the outfit she was proposing to wear. His fear was that she would be seen by his classmates as overdressed. They would call her 'posh' and he wouldn't know how to answer.

Now this old woman in the middle of the group had her face turned up to the sky and seemed oblivious to the fact that she was wearing a grey three-quarter-length raincoat over navy slacks and flat-heeled cream shoes. The shoes made her seem tiny, as did the fact that she was looking up at the sky. Had her bones begun to settle? Was she growing downwards?

The shuffling line at the other side of the road was almost level with him. He certainly didn't want to be seen, so he stooped to tie his shoelace, turning his face away. As the old people passed in their crocodile, all he heard was the scuffing of their feet and the occasional encouragement from one of the nurses. In order to tie his lace he had to lay the flowers on the ground. He was *not* content to mime, which would have been sufficient, but he actually wanted to *be* tying his lace. It was his mother who had taught him how to do this. A simple over and under, to start. Then a loop. Then another. 'Hey presto,' was what she always said when he finished. He risked looking across. Still none of the old people were talking. A blackbird sang. The caravan was now past. Where were they heading? It could only be the shops. He straightened up and looked after them as they walked towards the main road.

He carried on towards the Home. He didn't want to lose Brownie points by not showing his face. The Sister-in-charge, the one he knew and had had dealings with, might be on duty. He pressed the buzzer and it caused heads to turn in the entrance hall. A woman attendant came forward and opened the door. He gave his name, then his mother's name. Would it be possible to see her? The attendant brought him in and went off into an office. He stood in the middle of the carpeted space. It looked like a conservatory. Old people were asleep in their arm-chairs around the perimeter. Some were awake and began whispering to others, guessing who he was and who he was visiting. A tape of Irish country-and-western music played softly in the background. The attendant came back and apologised.

'Your mother's gone out for a little stroll – with some of the others. We thought it was such a nice day.'

'How long will she be?'

'Difficult to say. Depends . . . '

He didn't want to turn around and go. That way, nobody would know he had made the effort – that he'd put himself out. Could he see the Sister-in-charge? There were some matters he would like to discuss.

The attendant indicated a row of empty chairs. He laid the flowers across them and sat down, then eased his shoulder out from the strap of his bag. The old women across the hallway were nodding, smiling at him. All seemed to have had their white hair crimped and pompa-doured that morning. A man with horn-rimmed spectacles stared into the vault of the roof. Some people had Zimmer frames parked where they sat. It was a double-edged sword, his mother being in a Home like this. It stopped him worrying about her. Although it started him worrying about his own callousness in putting her there. But what could he do? He lived in another country. She had said that there was no way she was moving.

On one occasion he'd been visiting her in her own house. She was cutting bread for him, making him a bit of toast even though it was the middle of the day. The bread knife was one that had seen better times. She'd dropped it on the cooker ring and the plastic handle had melted a little. It was 'no longer fit for purpose'. However, she continued to use it, day in, day out, ignoring the scarred handle. He watched her closely as she cut the loaf, a bloomer, bought especially for his visit. She herself ate white pan bread

– said she refused to eat any kind of bread that bled her gums. As she sawed, the table vibrated on its thin tapered legs. She covered the bread and the knife with her other hand to steady and guide it. When the slice was cut, she dropped it into the toaster.

He was always short of ideas for presents, so on her next birthday he'd arrived with an expensive new bread knife. One side of the blade was for meat and the other for bread. It was the Ferrari of bread knives, he told her. But she cut herself slicing a sandwich, being used to resting her steadying hand on top of the knife. It left a red line across the undersides of three of her fingers, and a sandwich covered in blood. Until her wounds healed, she washed the dishes wearing one rubber glove.

Eventually the woman attendant came back and told him that Sister would see him now. He gathered himself and his bag and his flowers and followed her into the office.

'A vase for these,' said Sister to the attendant. Sister looked up at him and smiled. 'So you've missed her, it seems.'

'Yes.' For the third time that day he was conscious of a blackbird singing. The Sister was younger than he was. She was not in uniform but wore a stylish grey suit with a bright ceramic necklace.

'You said you had matters you wanted to discuss.'

'No . . . no.' He paused. 'I don't get over very often. I certainly intend to but . . . '

'The spirit is willing . . . '

'I was just wondering how she was getting on.'

'Very well.'

'Good.' There was silence. Then he said, 'Every time I come, she seems upset that she can't make me a cup of tea.'

Sister inclined her head and puckered her mouth a little.

'There's a small kitchen on every landing. But sometimes they think they're a lot more capable than they really are. In a place this size, we have to at least *nod* to Health and Safety. Can you imagine – all that boiling water?'

'I understand.'

'She's a woman of strong opinions, your mother. I mean, she's not backward about coming forward.'

'Never was.'

They smiled at each other – then Sister said, 'She thinks we're stealing from her.'

'That was on her mind the last time I was here.'

'And she says it out loud. But many of our patients make the same complaint. It's why we don't allow them a lot of money. A few pound coins in a purse to make them feel . . . you know. Grown-up. Your mother's very fond of her charity shops.'

'So I've noticed.'

'But they just set their purses down somewhere. Then the purse becomes "stolen".' She marked the air with her fingers to indicate punctuation.

'It was more her clothes she was complaining about.'

'Every item is labelled,' said the Sister. 'Laundry is taken and returned by hand.'

'She says a wolf could come in here and end up looking like a sheep.'

They both laughed.

And as the laughter died away Sister said, 'Good but not true.' Her hand went to her ceramic beads, as if to check they were still there. She then launched into a report. His mother, she found, was affable, friendly, kindly, but not a great mixer, staying away from communal activities – like bingo and sing-songs. But of course these things were voluntary.

He looked over Sister's shoulder at the ribbed windowpane. There was movement outside – then the beeping sound of a lorry reversing. The place was warm and he'd been up far too early that morning for his flight. He lost the thread of what she was saying. He was nodding. Like the meeting with the boss. Then she had stopped talking and was looking at him, as if waiting for a reply. Had she asked him a question? He looked down at his watch.

'I should really be on my way,' he said. 'I've a plane to catch.'

'It's such a shame to miss her. She'll be *so* disappointed when she hears.'

'I might catch up with her.' He was now standing, putting on his bag. 'I presume they've gone to the shops.'

'Yes. You couldn't miss them.'

At the shops on the main road a flash of white from one of the nurses' uniforms caught his eye.

'Excuse me,' he said. 'I've just been to the Home and they told me I could catch up with you here.' He explained who he was and said his mother's name.

'She was here just a moment ago,' said the nurse. 'I'll ask my colleague . . . ' She stepped between parked cars to consult the other nurse, who looked over at him. She must have recognised him from a previous visit because she waved at him. A small wave.

'She's in Madden's,' said the second nurse. 'The vegetable shop.'

'I haven't much time – I'll just say hello.'

In the greengrocer's at first he couldn't see her. He heard again the voice of the man serving.

'Lovely day.'

Then he saw his mother bending over, rummaging among the produce. When she straightened, he could see she had opened the buttons of her raincoat. She was wearing a powder-blue jumper with glitter – like something a *Big Issue* seller would wear. She had set a pot of jam on a shelf to leave her hands free and was trying to select the best onion from a box of onions. Weighing one in her hand, squeezing it, giving it the once-over. Showing off, to all and sundry, that she knew about onions. The outer skin flaked away and – still keeping its rounded shape – fell among the other empty skins. She plucked a thin polythene bag from a dispenser and stood there, trying to open it. She blew on it, tried to fiddle it open. Her tongue came out and she moistened a trembling finger.

He walked over to her and put on a voice. 'Can I help you with that, madam?'

She looked up at him, shaking her head.

'No, I'm fine. I've got a pot of jam – just in case anybody calls – and I'm looking for what'll make a drop of soup.' Then she recognised him. Her eyes widened and she half laughed, half gasped. 'What in the name of God are you doing here, son?'

'Visiting *you*.' He bent over and kissed her on the forehead and put his arms around her. 'But you weren't in residence.' She *was* growing downwards. He was aware of her head only coming up to his chest. She nuzzled into him. Then stood back off him, to take him in and reassure herself.

'It's like I'm dreaming you're here.' Then she began to call one or two of the other old people in the party to come over and meet her son. Three of them clustered round, looking up and smiling. The old woman in the middle had dentures that were too big for her. They all talked about him as if he wasn't there.

'He's gorgeous.'

'Isn't he very attentive.'

'Look at the height of him.'

He wondered if he should shake hands with each of them but in the end he didn't. His mother edged him away from them, as if she didn't want to share him any more. She still had an onion in one hand and the thin polythene bag in the other. The women called across the shop.

'Lovely to meet you.'

'Such a lovely man.'

'Who is he?'

'It's her boy.'

'Oh, I didn't realise.'

He turned his back on the old women and spoke to his mother.

'How are things?'

'Fine. I'm just getting something here to make a drop of soup.'

'Good for you.'

'Of course they make it easy nowadays. Look.' She produced a small cellophane pack and showed him. 'Soup mix,' she said. 'Barley, split peas and what-have-you. Everything. There's no bother making soup nowadays.'

'There never was.' He could just see it. As a boy he'd loved the pinhead globules of gold – all over the surface. 'I didn't think you'd be allowed.'

His mother stared at him, not understanding. She looked again with some dissatisfaction at the onion in her hand and dropped it back among the others.

'I just need a good onion and that'll be me finished.' She leaned over the tray of onions again and began lifting and feeling and choosing. He looked around him. The other old women were still staring at him.

'Mother – for God's sake – one onion's much like another.'

'You'd be surprised. At this time of year you get them home and cut them open and they're useless.' She picked up another. 'I'll not be a minute.'

'I don't have that much time. I've a flight to catch.'

'Oh, don't be late on my behalf, son.' She pulled a face, then picked an onion and put it in the poly bag. 'Soup is like me – it improves with age. First day's is watery. The next's better, but the third day's the real thing.' She also inserted a carrot and some leeks into the bag.

He asked her, 'Do you not get soup where you are?'

'It comes out of a tin the size of a drum. And you can taste the tin off it. It repeats on me all night. Gives me terrible water-brash.'

'Are you allowed to cook?'

'I never get the time. There's so much to be done.'

'Maybe you should give it a miss. This time.' He reached out and took the pot of jam and the poly bag from her.

'Health and Safety,' he said. He turned his back on her and crammed everything into his shoulder bag. She did not seem to miss her purchases. He took her by the elbow and edged her out of the shop onto the pavement.

'I was in here earlier and bought you some flowers.'

'What?'

'I went down to the . . . I went down to your place but you'd just gone. So they'll be in a vase for you when you get back.'

'What will?'

'The flowers I bought you. I've a flight to catch, so I'd better get my skates on.' He extended his arms and she came into them, nuzzled against him.

'Bye-bye, son. It was lovely to see you.'

'I'll be over again as soon as I can.' He kissed the top of her head and squeezed her shoulders. In daylight he could see through to her shining scalp. One of the nurses was nearby and she saw the leave-taking and came over. She manoeuvred the old woman into the group she was trying to muster. She passed him as she went to collect someone else.

'It's worse than herding sheep,' she said.

He nodded and hurried back into the shop.

'Lovely day,' said the greengrocer.

Rather than go around the shop replacing the items his mother had chosen, he paid for them and stuffed them into his shoulder bag.

'I'm in a bit of a rush,' he said. 'I've a flight to catch.'

In the taxi he kept looking at his watch. And each time he looked, he knew he shouldn't have. Because it was no help. The time would pass whether they were moving or stuck in traffic. He had never seen the airport road so jammed. Only one lane of three seemed to be moving. The driver's eyes looked at him in the mirror.

'What time did you say your flight was?'

He told him again. The driver looked round and began to signal.

'Musta been an accident.'

He edged across to the inside lane, danced the car in and out of the hard shoulder, pretending to wave thanks to drivers he'd put under pressure to admit him.

'You should make it okay. If you run . . . '

He was grateful he'd already checked in online. He ran across the concourse straight to security. The screens told him yet again what he should be doing. With his coat, his mobile, his laptop, his belt. What he should be doing with his liquids even. Everyone seemed to take ages. Shuffling forward, kicking their bags along the tiled floor. He looked at his watch yet again and wondered if the airline would close the gate. In the papers he'd read of a couple who'd sued because they'd missed their flight, despite arriving at the airport two hours before take-off. What was utterly stupid was that, as far as he knew, there was no communication whatsoever between security and the flight desks. It could be an overcrowded day, with everybody being searched at a snail's pace, and the flight desk would know nothing about it. Take-off would still be at the same time.

When it came to his turn, he unsheathed his laptop and set it in the plastic tray. As he was zipping the shoulder bag closed, he remembered. They would not like it, wouldn't like it at all. It could take for ever sorting it out and he would miss his flight. He was waved through and had to stand in a booth like Vitruvian Man while security searched him. Arms, chest, waist, thighs, ankles.

When he was cleared, he stood waiting for his tray to break through the hanging straps of the X-ray tunnel. A uniformed security man held up a bag.

'Looks like mine.'

He was nodded over to the metal tables.

'Mind if I take a look?'

These bastards had people where they wanted them. If they refused or made a fuss, they'd miss their flight. So everything was a nod of the head. Yes, go right ahead.

'Can you open the bag for me, sir?'

He opened the zip. The security man was wearing white rubber gloves and delved into the various recesses. He produced the plastic bag containing the onion, the leeks, the carrot and the sachet. The leeks had black soil around their roots. He held the bag up to the light.

'It's okay,' said the security man. 'It's just that we don't see it very often.'

'What?'

'Soup makings.'

'They even include free soup mix.'

'So I see.' The security man raised an eyebrow, rummaged deeper and produced a pot of jam.

'This is definitely not allowed,' he said. 'Classified as a liquid.'

'It's jam.'

'It's a gel and it's not allowed.'

'A present from my mother.'

He knew it was a lie, but figured the man in uniform wouldn't pursue his line of questioning. The security guy turned away and walked to a sink. On his way he popped the lid. He upended the jar and its contents glugged into a red heap in the sink. What an utterly futile gesture. And, as he stood there waiting, the futility somehow transferred to his mother. Her shrinking face, that charity-shop raincoat with its sloped shoulders, her sequinned clothes, her irreversible plight. She would not have stood for such waste. And if it had been a different place, he might have cried. He clenched his teeth against the urge.

The security man ran the tap and washed the mess down the plughole, then dropped the jar into a bin, which, by the sound of it, was full of other glass items. He came back and gestured that the computer could now be stowed. He looked closely at him.

'All right, sir?'

As a sign of his friendliness, the security man slid the vegetables in beside the anodised aluminium of the laptop and indicated that the passenger was free to go and catch his plane home.

SEARCHING

Belfast 1971

She didn't know what woke her. It must have been something. She switched on the bedside light and saw it was just after three. Switched off again and lay rigid in the darkness. The return room was silent. Its single window, open a fraction for summer air, overlooked the back lane and yard. Not even the bark of a dog in the distance. She didn't usually wake in the middle of the night and thought there must be some explanation. Maybe it was in answer to a prayer. If Mammy, sleeping up in the front bedroom, had taken ill and prayed aloud, it was Molly's duty to check on her. One short flight of stairs above. Put her head round the door. Maybe no need even for this. The old woman might be snoring and she could hear her from the landing.

It was one of the things she hated about being a widow woman, this feeling of being scared. Not that her husband, when he was alive, could have done very much about it, but at least she would have known he was there. Fear shared was fear reduced. She slept soundly the couple of nights her son came home from London.

But now she was a sixty-year-old, totally in charge. And yet she knew she was incapable of being in charge of anything, never mind her mother – all eighty-three years of her. She could deal with ordinary things, like putting meals on the table. Or walking her slowly round the corner to half-ten Mass on a Sunday. Or if the Hoover gave up, she could ask her brother-in-law, who had skills in that direction, to fix it. That kinda stuff was all right. But noises, enough to wake you in the middle of the night, in a town such as this, were a different matter altogether. She lay completely still, not to confuse the sounds of the bedclothes with sounds from elsewhere. Or the noise of the mattress as her body pressurised it. Then she heard a sound. Definitely. The smallest imaginable. That 's' sound some people make when praying. A lisp. More a whisper than a voice. It sounded like it had come up through the barely-open window. Someone in the yard, maybe. Mother-a-God, what was it? She now lifted her head off the pillow to free both ears. Lay facing up to the dark of the ceiling. She'd noticed the cat, when she was alert about something, moving her ears like radar, following a sound. That was her now. It was not people talking, but it could be people whispering. And why would anyone want to be whispering outside – why not just talk? She couldn't make it out. Then she definitely heard something.

Breaking glass. Jesus, Mary and Joseph. On two separate occasions her windows had been blown in by bombs, but here – now – there had been no explosion. And there was a clanging sound like it was big bits of glass that were being broken. It was coming from the front of the house downstairs. Somebody's throwing bricks through the windows at three in the morning. But also bumping noises. Breaking sounds. Christ the night. She switched on her bedside lamp and got into her dressing gown. She was shaking. Her legs almost gave way beneath her. She hadn't time to tie the belt of her dressing gown before the bumping sounds were coming up the carpeted stairs, getting nearer. Shouting voices. Fast footsteps, pounding.

'Who is it?' Her voice quavered so much she had to say it again. Louder. 'Who is it?'

'British Army, mam.'

'Aw – thanks be to God.'

She opened the bedroom door a fraction. The place was alive with soldiers carrying guns. They had taken the liberty to turn on all the lights downstairs. About five or six of them. The cat streaked away from them up the stairs with a kind of terrified speed. The big front door was just the way she had left it when she'd locked up earlier.

'How did you get in?'

One soldier sprinted past her room on his way upstairs. She was aware of the grey-black gun in his arms and the gills along the side of it. The man in front of her, who seemed to be in charge, shouted into her face.

'I want everyone in the house downstairs. Now!'

'You'll scare the wits out of my mother,' she yelled at the squaddie running upstairs. He kicked open the back bedroom door with the sole of his boot and disappeared. Her mother was in the other room, the front room.

'I'll get her up,' she shouted and jostled past the first soldier up the stairs. He made a vain attempt to stop her and direct her downstairs but he seemed to have no hands left. 'Mammy, Mammy.' The old woman's bedroom door was always left slightly open – just in case. In case she called out in the night, in case she needed help with something, in case she had another attack. In case the cat needed a place of refuge.

'Is that you, Molly?'

'It's me.'

She hurried in the door. The light was on. Her mother was sitting up in bed with the sheets bunched up in her fist beneath her chin. The cat was nowhere to be seen.

'What in the name of God is going on?' said the old woman. 'Who's shouting?'

The soldier-in-charge stepped into the room behind her. He apologised for the disturbance, but said it was necessary. And that he wanted everybody in the house downstairs, where he could keep an eye on them. Molly heard someone run past her mother's room and pound up the stairs to the top of the house. Loud voices with no laughing. That was scary. She knew what they would find up there. Because she alone knew what she was guilty of.

'Excuse me,' called Molly and she opened the door wide and followed whoever it was who had gone upstairs. 'Oh, merciful hour.' She knew every tread. Every squeak and creak. Her heart was pounding and her breath came in gasps as she climbed as quickly as she could.

The soldier-in-charge had come out onto the landing. He was shouting up to her that he wanted the occupants downstairs. Now. Where he could see them. Molly thought he was just afraid to be left alone with her mother in the bed.

The squaddie ahead had pushed the front top bedroom door open. Molly followed him in. The curtains were not pulled and the street lights dimly lit the place from outside. She switched on the bedroom light. The soldier was down on his knees at the bedside. He had his arm thrust beneath the rumpled covers of the unmade bed.

'What are you doing?' She was breathless, after the stairs. He withdrew his arm, ignored her and stood. He lifted the ashtray on the bedside table. There were a couple of cigarette ends in it. Her son had never been able to give them up. The soldier smelled them, touched them with his fingers. He was only a boy, really, but his face was streaked with blackening. He looked up to the ceiling. He stood like that for a while. When he spoke with his head back, his Adam's apple moved. It was white. He had not blackened it. His voice was shaky.

'Isthereaceilinghatch, mam?'

'Sorry?'

'A ceilinghatch?'

'I don't understand you. And I don't understand what you're doing.'

He pointed up as if she was a child.

'An atch. In the ceiling. An escape atch.'

'No. Only in the bathroom. For the water tank.'

The soldier-in-charge came into the room. He too looked up at the ceiling. Then at the bed.

'Who's been sleeping here?'

'My son.'

'Where is he?'

'He went back to London.'

'When?'

'Two weeks ago.' The soldier-in-charge slid his free hand into the bed.

'Why's the bed not made up?'

She shrugged.

'I dunno.'

'For two weeks?'

'I'm so busy with my mother . . . just never got round to it. It's at the top of the house. What business is it of yours?'

He also became interested in the ashtray, which was just a white saucer. He smelled and felt the cigarette ends. Then he left the room and went downstairs. The other, younger guy nodded and walked to the wall cupboard. He wrenched it open. She knew what was in it – it was where she stored anything and everything useless. An old radio that didn't work, picture frames with broken glass, her son's cricket pads – he always said he was a better bat than a bowler – roller blinds, bamboo canes, threadbare rugs that it would have ashamed her to put down on the floor. The soldier toppled some of the things out to look behind them.

'How dare you! Have you no manners?'

The soldier boy said something under his breath but she couldn't make out what it was. It didn't sound complimentary. He walked past her out of the room and went down the stairs two at a time. Into the bathroom. She watched him go. He pulled the light-switch cord and looked up at the ceiling. Before she followed him down, she turned her attention to the bed. She straightened the undersheet and tucked it beneath the mattress. Then the blankets. Then the pink-satin eiderdown. All the time she was making a moaning noise. 'Aw no, aw no.' She left the mess the squaddie had toppled out of the cupboard, stepped over it all.

She followed him down to the bathroom, holding tightly onto the banister. He had closed and bolted the bathroom door. God knows what he was up to. The soldier-in-charge was elsewhere.

She continued on down to her mother's bedroom.

When she came in, she clasped her hair to her head and said, 'I'm mortified. Utterly mortified.'

'What's wrong? Are they still here?' the old woman said from the bed. 'I can't hear them.' Molly nodded. 'But then I can't hear very much anyway.'

She saw her mother's hands outside the sheets, thumbing through her beads.

'I'm saying the rosary, so's they'll go. And go soon.'

'What are they looking for?'

'It'll be somebody on the run.'

'That sounds very old-fashioned.'

'Like the twenties,' said her mother. 'When we moved in here we were told the roof space runs the length of the terrace.'

'Would you like a cuppa tea?'

Her mother thought about this. Then nodded her head – yes. 'It'll put me off my sleep. But then so will all this.' In the faint light of the table lamp, the skin on the back of her mother's hands shone.

'Up here or downstairs?' said Molly.

'What?'

'Maybe we should go downstairs. The man in charge seems very insistent.' Molly helped her mother out of bed.

The old woman pulled her nightdress as far down as it would go. Molly stripped a cover off the bed and draped it over her mother's shoulders. 'Next time I'm in town I'm buying you a dressing gown.'

'I'm like a shawlie coming outta the mill,' her mother said. Molly took the opportunity to tie the belt of her own dressing gown. A quick whirl of her hands, a tightening at her waist.

'That's us. Ready for the road.'

But her mother turned back for her black trunk of a handbag.

'Oh, Mother, will you come on.'

The old woman handfulled her rosary beads into the bag and snapped the clasp shut. She hung it over her right forearm. On the stairs she kept her balance with her other hand on the banister. Molly preceded her going down, broadened her own back in case her mother should fall. The sitting-room door was open and she felt the cold draught coming from the room. She looked in – the window was smashed, including the frame, a rectangle of tilted wood and broken glass. Her good net curtains ballooned, looked like they were torn to bits.

'How in under God am I going to get that fixed?' she said.

In the hall her mother stood waiting. Soldiers weaved around her.

'Come on, Mammy.' Molly led her to her armchair and sat her down. A soldier was standing on a wooden stool, going through a high cupboard. 'You'll find damn all up there.'

There were two other soldiers outside in the yard – one was in the coalhouse, the other was bent over searching through a bin with a torch. At that precise moment the kitchen was empty.

'Would you like a cup of tea now?'

The soldier on the stool looked round. 'Thank you, mam. Very nice of you,' he said.

'Catch yourself on. I was talking to my mother.'

The soldier pulled a face, which admitted he'd made a mistake – a kind of Oops.

'Maybe hot milk would be better for you,' said Molly to her mother. 'Help you sleep.' Molly half filled a small saucepan with milk and put it on the gas. The soldier-in-charge came into the room and nodded a greeting towards the old lady in the armchair. He seemed to have calmed down a bit. He went out to check on the two guys in the yard. Light from the torch fell on the etched kitchen window now and again. Voices from the yard were indistinct. The soldier-in-charge came back in again. The squaddie, still standing on the stool, looked round.

'Look what I found,' he said and tossed something across the room. The soldier-in-charge caught it expertly with one hand and held it up. A cricket ball – red as a cherry. With a white sewn seam. He rubbed it on the front of his fatigue pants as if he was shining it in the middle of a game.

'Hey,' he said. 'Like the day it was bought.' His face lit up. He looked between the women for some explanation.

'That's my son's,' said Molly from the cooker. 'Put it back, if you don't mind.'

'Does he play?'

Molly nodded. She seemed reluctant to become involved in a conversation. But the man's voice was very posh – it lured her in. Like something from the BBC. He brought the cricket ball up to his face and smelled it, and a look passed over his blacked features.

'Who does he play for?'

'Just a local team. He used to go up the Cliftonville Road.'

'Does he still play?'

'In England?'

'Yes.'

'I believe so. I've a photo of him somewhere, wearing whites. And the pad-things.'

The man-in-charge continued polishing the ball. He shook his head slowly, as if in disbelief.

'Who does he play for in England?'

'Is this an interrogation?'

'No, it's a conversation. Who for?'

'How would I know? West Ham? Fulham Wanderers? God knows.'

There was a loud hissing noise as the milk foamed up and boiled over.

'Now look what you've made me do.'

Molly moved the saucepan away from the heat. She poured the hot milk into a cup, then added a little cold milk from the bottle.

'Here.' She carried it to her mother. 'That'll not keep you awake.'

The old woman beckoned her down with her eyebrows. Molly leaned close. Her mother whispered, 'Why are you talking to him so much?'

'Och,' Molly said and straightened up.

Her mother blew on the surface of the milk and sipped it cautiously. Molly went back to the cooker to clean up the mess.

'I thought Roman Catholics didn't play cricket,' said the soldier-in-charge as she passed him. He was still polishing the ball slowly on his trousers. He held it up to look at the shine, then laid his index finger along the seam as if he was going to spin the ball.

Molly hesitated. 'That shows you how little you know,' she said.

And then they were gone. Just as suddenly as they'd arrived. And over the following days and weeks, no matter how hard she looked, she could never find her son's cricket ball.

NIGHT WORK

She had just taken her biscuit from the tin and was warming some milk for her supper when she heard the front door – the little brass hand clacking. Who on earth was calling at this hour? It was almost bedtime. She took the milk off the gas. The knocking came again. Given the lateness of the hour, she thought she'd better check before opening the door.

Even when she held the curtain to one side she could not see properly. The frost had covered the inside of the glass with feathers. She rubbed a hole in the grey patterns with the flat of her hand. The person outside in the pitch dark was a man. He seemed agitated, stepping from one foot to the other. Maybe he had mistaken the address. Maybe he would go away? With the movement of the curtain, the light from her window fell across him and he looked in her direction. He knocked a third time. Then she recognised him. It was the boy who lived across the landing from the sculptor. The woman shuffled to the front door and opened it.

'What's wrong?'

The boy was shivering and it made his speech difficult to understand. He had no coat, just a knitted jumper against the cold.

'Nothing,' he said. 'He has a job for you.'

'Who?'

'The sculptor.'

'Can it not wait?'

He handed her a page torn from a notebook, jagged along one side. His hand was shaking badly with the cold. She took it from him and had to step back into the hallway, so the light from her room shone on the paper. Her hallway breathed out a mist into the night.

'Come in,' she said without raising her eyes as she read. The boy stepped inside. His lips were blue and his face ashen, drained of any colour by the cold.

'He says he can't do it himself,' said the boy.

'Why not?'

'He busted his foot.'

'When? I saw him two days ago and he was fine.'

'Well, he's not now.'

'How'd he do that?'

'A gas cylinder fell on him.'

'One of the big rusty ones?'

The boy nodded.

'I'll bet he was mad,' she said. But she was smiling. The boy had closed over the door to keep out the cold and was leaning against the wall.

'He was hopping mad.'

'You and your jokes. Let me get ready and I'll come round with you. There's stuff I need from there.'

She went back into her room, leaving the boy in the dark of the hallway.

'I'll not be long,' she raised her voice, so as he could hear.

When she came out she was dressed for the weather. Buttoned overcoat – stout shoes, woollen scarf and a black hat pulled down well over her ears. She was carrying a hessian bag on her forearm.

'Maybe you want to run on ahead,' she said. 'You look foundered.'

'Naw, I'm okay.' He thrust his hands into his trouser pockets and continued to walk beside her.

'I suppose he's like a bear with a sore head.'

'Sore foot, more like.' She could see his breath when he laughed.

'Did he give you any money?'

'Naw – not yet.'

'Well, make sure he does. Coming out at this time.' She was now panting a little. The youth, although he'd refused to run ahead, was now setting a pace faster than she was used to. He must want back to the heat of his home.

The tenement was not far away and they were there in five minutes. Once inside the hallway, they created echoes up into the stairwell – the door slamming, their footsteps on the terrazzo floor. The boy leapt the stone stairs two at a time, then waited for her. When she reached the first landing he nodded politely, said goodnight and went to the left. She let herself into the door opposite with her keys.

In the dark she found the light switch just as she did on cleaning mornings.

'Hello? Lily?'

The voice was from the sculptor's bedroom. His light came on and, to give him time to make himself decent, she tapped the wood panel of the door with her fingernail.

'Come ahead.' She pushed on the door and it swung open.

'It's only me,' she said.

'I can't sleep with the pain.' He was in bed, except for his foot, which stuck out from the bottom of the eiderdown. The foot was blue with cold or injury, she couldn't tell which. There was a majolica chamberpot on the bedside chair. From where she stood, she could not see if it had been used. Nor did she want to see.

'I hear you were in a fight with a cylinder,' she said. He rolled his eyes to the ceiling.

'It was my own fault. There's twenty-six bones in the human foot and I feel I've broken every bloody one of them.'

'What did the doctor say?'

'I didn't go. It'll be all right in a day or two. By that time, I'll have made myself a crutch.'

'So?'

'Sorry to disturb you at this hour,' said the sculptor. 'Earlier on this evening I had a visit from an old friend.'

'Who?'

'A well-off woman from my past. She wanted to commission me, but with this bloody foot I couldn't accept. And then I remembered you, Lily.'

She set her bag on the floor and inched her hip onto the bed. It must be important if he was calling her Lily. He was wheedling, almost.

'Will I be paid?' she asked.

'Yes, yes. I'd've done it myself, but for this.' He nodded to the bed foot.

'Could it not wait until tomorrow?'

'The sooner it's done, the better. Better to get in before anybody else. Before anybody can make things look false. God knows, maybe even smiling.' He laughed. 'So get your skates on. You know where everything is.'

She nodded.

'I'll not be a minute.'

She went into the walk-in store cupboard off the studio and began to rummage. A cut-throat razor. Stacked newspapers, with God knows what dates. Soap. She checked the plaster was still useable. The old chipped tin mug he used for a scoop moved freely through it. Sometimes the stuff solidified, unbeknownst. This place was damp but he claimed never to be able to afford repairs.

'Don't forget the Vaseline,' he shouted from the bed.

'As if I would.'

When she returned to the bedroom with her filled bag, his head above the eiderdown looked strange – as if someone had set it on the pillow to come back for it later – his greying Bismarck moustache, his nostrils of unequal size.

'Oh, and this. You might need this.' His arm emerged and picked up a purple envelope from the bedside table. It had a name and address sprawled across it in his distinctive Indian-ink handwriting. 'It explains who you are – why it's not me.' He offered it to her, putting on a pompous voice. 'Authority to carry out the procedure, and suchlike.' She stepped forward and took it, all the time averting her eyes from the chamberpot. 'The blackest of ink on an envelope of heliotrope,' said the sculptor, smiling.

'I hope that wasn't there when her ladyship was in.' She nodded at the pot.

'You cannot imagine how important this is,' he said. 'Cash *and* kudos. It could get us remembered. Even when we're all dead and gone. My friend, she says he's a mathematician.' The sculptor was scratching his head, now that both his hands were free. 'Probably why nobody seems to have heard of him. Adam Smith he's not. Nor Hume nor bloody Boswell. I don't know what the world's coming to. To be famous for sums.'

'Do you want anything?' she said.

'I think I'm okay. I'll go over the process again, if you like.'

She rolled her eyes.

'One more thing,' he said. 'This is between ourselves. I wouldn't want the word to get out.'

She left before he could start talking again.

She knew the way because the address on the envelope was near the university. The streets were dark and silent and empty. The sculptor was always putting on the poor mouth. Art was a fool's game, he said. There was more money in being a bank clerk than in sculpture. But she knew he had money. In properties. He rented her the ground-floor room she lived in. This meant he rarely, if ever, had to pay her for her labour. He owned the flat he lived in, and the one across the landing where the shivering boy lived with his family. In the twenties and early thirties he'd sold pieces of sculpture all over Europe.

Either the temperature had risen or the exercise of walking had warmed her. She came to a gradual hill and angled herself to climb it. After a while she stopped to get her breath back and undo the button at her throat. She turned around to see how far she had climbed and saw the bright moon over the vast sea loch behind her. It created a reflection all the way across the water, like a lit roadway. There were clouds on the horizon that seemed full of snow. In the light of the moon, the hills in front of her looked like icebergs.

But there was no wind and the air seemed to magnify the sounds around her. The soft rasp of her bag against the material of her coat, the sound of a single motor car climbing another hill nearby, her shoes scratching on the grit of the pavement. They were good shoes – belonged to the woman who'd lived next door. But she'd died last year and, after the funeral, her daughter had given them to her. They were on the big side, but that was better than being too small. With cramped footwear you could end up compensating or walking funny. Or developing corns. When shoes were on the big side, a little newspaper padding helped. Polished up, these ones still looked good. Compact, sturdy, not unstylish. They gave her a good grip of the ground. Gave her confidence.

After the small station she turned left. Even at this time of the evening, stations were dangerous places for a woman on her own. Doorways seemed darker, sounds more ominous. A laugh could not be taken at face value. Railway lines curved away in the moonlight. She took the envelope from her bag to reacquaint herself with the house number.

The avenue was tree-lined, the houses set well back off the roadway. The foliage threw dark shadows onto the pavement. House numbers were displayed on only some of the gate pillars. It was so dark beneath the trees that she became wary with each stride. There were wet leaves underfoot, damping the noise of her footfall. She found the house number she was looking for on the ornamental stone gateway. It was cold to the touch as her fingers confirmed the digits. She swung open the iron gate and it squeaked. The garden looked overgrown with bracken and dried grasses. Her hand felt around for a bell or knocker. It was a sort of metallic wing nut or butterfly. She turned it and a sound, halfway between a rasp and a ring, startled her. No one came – she waited a polite length of time. It would be a house in mourning, after all. She twisted the mechanical bell again. It seemed louder the second time. Or else she was becoming more agitated.

A shadow moved in the hallway, approaching the grey glass of the door. The young man who opened it nodded and leaned forward as if he was hard of hearing. She said – rather too loudly – that she had been sent by the sculptor to carry out a commission and held out the purple envelope.

'Come in,' he said. 'Have a seat.' He indicated an upright chair in the hallway. She sat down and the young man walked away. There were quiet voices in the distance. A faint clash of china plates. Cutlery being dropped into a drawer. The walls from floor to ceiling were covered with pictures – paintings, photographs, framed posters. There was an accumulation of dust on each of them. Grey on the top and bottom lip of the frame. A feather duster was required. There were books everywhere – bookcases lined the walls and books, for which there was no room, accumulated on the stairs. They were piled on each tread, next to the wall, so that they formed another staircase of books as they went upwards.

A woman appeared with the letter in her hand and looked into the hall. She was in her late fifties, early sixties. It was obvious she had been crying.

'I hadn't expected you to be a woman,' she said. They shook hands and the woman of the house indicated the stairs. There was a red carpet held in place with brass stair-rods. Both women climbed slowly and quietly.

'The doctor has already been here,' said the woman of the house. 'So there is no need to worry about that.'

'And the undertaker?'

'He'll come in the morning.'

At the head of the stairs was a grandfather clock. The dial was painted with moons and suns and golden stars.

'You have a lovely house.'

'It's not ours. It belongs to our friends. We haven't been here very long.' The woman of the house didn't sound local. Not from these parts at all. Her English was perfect but accented. But Lily couldn't figure out where she was from, and these days it could be an awkward question to ask. The woman of the house led the way along a landing and opened a door. The room was dimly illuminated by a red bedside lamp. A woman in an overcoat and scarf was sitting at the foot of the bed. She turned around to see who was coming in, and her spectacles reflected what little light there was. The woman with the spectacles stood.

'Excuse me,' she said. 'I'll just slip down for a cup of tea.'

'I'm sure you are thirsty, love,' said the woman of the house.

She stood aside and as the woman with the specs went out the door, she patted her.

'We're not religious,' said the woman of the house, 'but I always want to have somebody in the room with him. It's the way they do things at home. I'm sorry I've forgotten your name.' She held the letter up, as if in an apology.

'Lily.'

'When something like this happens, Lily, you can think of little else.'

The dead man lay on the bed beneath the quilt. His head rested on a low pillow.

'I'm sorry for your trouble,' said Lily. 'What was he to you?'

'My husband. I'm not sure I should have agreed to this.'

'Well . . . '

'But she is a very persuasive woman, the woman who asked for this. It's hard to say no to her. She has money.' The woman of the house rubbed her fingers and thumb together to indicate just how much. Lily was unsure how to react. She made as if to turn and go.

'But I suppose he is beyond harm.' The woman of the house began to cry. Lily reached out and touched her elbow. The woman seemed grateful for the gesture and nodded her thanks. She pulled a handkerchief from her sleeve and wiped her mouth and nose.

'How long will you be?' she asked.

'An hour or so?' said Lily. 'Maybe two.'

'Can I get you anything?'

'Just some water.' Lily pointed to the ewer standing in a basin. 'That would do.' The woman of the house picked up the jug and went along the landing to the bathroom. Lily set her bag on a dresser and turned to look at the body. A man in his sixties – no moustache, which was a godsend. It was several days since he'd shaved. His features were sharp and birdlike. His skin colour between yellow and grey. Brown wear-marks from his spectacles on either side of his nose. There were several pairs of glasses on the bedside table. Distantly she heard the squeak of a tap and the roar of water into the ewer. The woman of the house came back and set the jug in the basin.

'Would you like some tea?'

'No, thank you. I'm fine.'

'We'll be sitting up most of the night anyway. In the kitchen. Maybe you'll take a cup before you leave. Or a glass of something.'

'You're very kind.' Lily began to unbutton her coat. The woman of the house bowed her head.

'I'm sorry, I can't watch this.' She turned and, before she left the room, she said, 'Go gentle on him. For I loved him very much.' She began to cry again but stifled it. Then she said, 'Everybody says he was a man of immense importance. To the whole wide world. But to me he was . . . ' She didn't finish her sentence, or else she was crying again. The door closed from the outside with a click.

✳

Lily relaxed. The books had invaded this room too. They lined the walls and had crept from the top of the bookcase onto the marble mantelpiece. On the hearth they were piled in uneven columns and looked like they could avalanche at any minute. She took off her hat and coat and laid them over an armchair. It was ages since she'd done any of this. But she was thrilled that the sculptor had entrusted her. She walked around the bed, sizing up the task. The floorboards squeaked beneath her weight. The room was so dim. She found the switch and turned on the overhead light. From her hessian bag she took newspapers and slid one between the dead man's head and the pillow. She lathered his lower face and shaved him as best she could, aware of the scratch noise the razor made at each sweep. There was a smell of stale sweat coming from him or his pyjamas. When finished, she dried his face with a towel. The man's skin had lost its spring and it was cold under her fingertips.

Some pillows and a bolster lay on a tallboy. She set the pillows by the headboard and eased the corpse upwards a little. The bolster she slid beneath his neck. Other newspapers she rolled as she would make paper sticks for the fire, and measured them for size against his face. Then she framed his face with the most firmly rolled one. Beneath this she created a bib of folded newspaper pages. She took a little tin of Vaseline petroleum jelly from her bag and daubed his hairline, his eyebrows.

In the beginning she had helped the sculptor make some masks of his own face. He had a great fear of suffocation and made her insert paper drinking straws into his nostrils so that he could continue to breathe in the period it took the plaster to dry. But this poor man was dead – had no more need of breathing. 'Where do we end?'

She spread layers of newspapers on the marble top of the dresser. The topmost one was recent – with headlines of the possibility of another war in Europe. She opened the round cake tin the sculptor used for mixing. Poured in a little water from the ewer and sprinkled on powder. Like the way she baked griddle-bread. She just knew how much to add, when to stir, when to mix. When to tap the sides of the tin to release air bubbles. When not to stir, as it would create new air bubbles. She felt the heat of the paste increase. When it was the right consistency, she lifted the tin onto the bed and began to coat the dead man's face with the mixture, beginning at his hairline. One or two rivulets of white trickled down onto the newspaper bib. But the mixture was thickening already. Care had to be taken with the hollows of the eyes. Bubbles could gather there. Make sure with the thumbs. And the nose. There was a great delicacy required with the nose – its sheer falling off, its cavernous nostrils. She had to work quickly – to cover the whole of the face to some depth in a couple of minutes. Her breathing was loud with the effort. Also the nervousness of wanting it to be right. She walked around the bed to see her work from all angles, to see if she had missed anything. Her hands she held away from herself and felt them tighten as the material dried. It was done – like a pale cowpat in the middle of the man's face, God love him.

She cleaned as much of the white muck off her hands as she could. To anyone who asked, she explained the process in terms of photography – the plaster cast was the negative, the positive was what came out of it – an exact replica, be it of plaster or bronze. She wrapped some paper around the jug handle. A little fresh water into the basin to rinse her hands. The water paled and swirled, became like milk. She dried her hands and sat down on the chair where the woman with the glasses had been sitting. Then she realised she had no way of telling the time. Her watch, forgotten at home on her bedside table. She hated having the track of it on her wrist, so at night she took it off. In the sculptor's studio there had always been a clock on the wall for timings. She remembered the grandfather clock in this house at the head of the stairs. She rose and went outside to the landing. A telephone rang in the distance. She tiptoed because she didn't want those downstairs to know she had left the dead man unattended. She could hear voices – then a man laughing. The chink of glasses, and then others joining in the laughter. The clock was so tall she had to look up.

How wondrous, she thought. Painted moons and suns and golden stars peered down from a night-blue sky. The hands were ornately curlicued, pointing to Roman numerals. It was almost the hour. There was a painting of St George and the dragon and a naked woman reclining on a rock. Waiting to be rescued or ravished. The reclining woman seemed uncertain herself. The clock chimed once.

Going back along to the room, she felt nervous, fearing the body might have disappeared or, even worse, come alive again. In some places in the Highlands when there was a death, the family removed a tile from the roof to let the soul of the deceased escape. Had this man's soul gone yet? The door squeaked as she opened it and she was almost afraid to look at the bed. But there he was, exactly as she'd left him. She sat down again.

A half an hour would do it. That was one of the good things about living by herself. She would disturb no one coming in at that hour of the morning. And she could sleep as long as she liked. As the sculptor had once said to her, 'If you get the reputation of rising early, you can lie in your bed till lunchtime.'

The sculptor was one of the few friends she'd made in the city when she'd first arrived twenty or so years ago. By asking around, she'd got herself a job in a café – at first washing dishes, then later waiting on tables. There was a man with extravagant black hair and matching moustache who sometimes came in for lunch. The first time she served him, she'd noticed wood chips snagged in his hair and thought he was a joiner or carpenter. The owner of the café explained that the man was a sculptor. 'A cheap chiseller' was the owner's mocking phrase.

Then, after a while of coming in and out of the café, the sculptor asked her if she would like to help him. He'd undertaken a series of works where he used himself as a model, and for that he needed another pair of hands. 'It's impossible for me to cast my own arm, for instance.' Then when that was a success, he went on to more complex, more complicated castings. She found it very difficult to know when anything was a success – Her only gauge of that was the sculptor's reaction. He would walk around and around the piece, touching and genuflecting. Crouching and squinting up his eyes. He was such a perfectionist. She would look at him, hoping for a hint on how to react.

He would nod and then, more often than not, would ask her to make some tea.

Depending on her shifts in the café, he would arrange for her to come and help him make casts of his hands, his feet, eventually his torso. 'Where do we end?' he kept saying. She learned to make and apply the plaster mixture to him. He was about ten years younger than her, with a lean and hairless body. What body hair he produced, he shaved, to save himself yelping at the plaster's removal. He needed other hands – hers – to extract him from the casting. 'Do we end at our skin? Or are we more than just that?' She neither knew nor cared what it was all about, as long as she got paid. Sometimes it meant seeing him naked – when he was casting his torso or lower body. She tried not to look because it embarrassed her. Especially if he showed signs of arousal. If this happened, he would laugh and turn his back to her and say it was just his body declaring a preference. Pointing her out, so to speak.

He eventually tired of this line of exploration in his work but liked her company. So he asked her to stay on and become his housekeeper two or three days a week – washing, sweeping, dusting. He forbade her to clean his studio – to touch anything in it. He'd had a bad experience with a previous woman cleaner – tidying, throwing things out. In the bin he'd found scraps of paper he'd drawn on, bits and pieces of wood and metal he'd been working on, maquettes and the like. Little things like conical shells, or bird skulls, went inexplicably missing. Her dismissal came after she was caught burning the crushed paper forms he'd been working on – the woman's tears when she tried to explain that she thought the stuff was packing material for some piece of sculpture – not the sculptural piece itself. So, on the days Lily was in, she washed dishes, cleaned his clothes as best she could, made an effort to tidy his bedroom, change his bed linen. Sweep and make presentable the kitchen and living room.

After a row with the owner, he deserted the café where Lily worked and went to a more popular place, where artists and the like gathered. Such people had no money and sometimes paid for meals with their work – paintings, drawings, sculptures.

As a consequence of the afternoons of body-casting, the sculptor became Lily's one and only lover. For a while, that is. The day it started, she had been watching him welding, the sparks raining onto the floor, bouncing but not burning – leaving no marks. Then he looked up at her. When they made love, the tracks of his blackened goggles were around his eyes. And his smile, always his smile, with his hair awry.

'Where do we begin? When do we end?'

Until eventually he tired of her. He was not a cruel man and tried to make up to her by offering her a room to rent, five minutes' walk away. Over the years, different lovers took her place and she found herself scrubbing sheets that were stained by the passion of others.

The whole evening had reminded her of how little time she had left. She was more than halfway through her life – more of an age with the man who'd died. She had smelled him, touched him, wondered briefly if what had caused his death could be infectious. She dismissed that idea. But she knew it was all before her. That some day she would die. It came for the famous and those who had no fame whatsoever. A consolation for many was being part of a lineage, but even this was denied her, having neither chick nor child to come after her. Her shoulders were beginning to stoop. Her skin was losing its ability to bounce back.

The grandfather clock chimed again on the half hour. She went to the bed and touched the plaster to check the hardening process was complete. She began to detach it, levering a little here, a little there. When it was free, she turned it over and looked for imperfections. Bubbles, creases, absence of wrinkles where the material had not insinuated itself. There were none that she could see. But the sculptor might take a different view. He was so pernickety, so arty. A real stickler. He saw things she wouldn't notice in a thousand years of looking. So, almost as an afterthought, she decided to do a second cast. To be on the safe side. She knew she could take another one from the first, but it was fiddly and could maybe cause some damage or distortion. As she worked, mixing and applying the second, it occurred to her that if the sculptor thought the first mask was valuable, then a second could also be worth something.

She left the wake-house and began to retrace her steps. Her shoes romped along and gave her reassurance. Their previous owner, her neighbour, was in the grave. So too, in a couple of days, would be the man whose images she had taken tonight. But *she* was not dead, and tomorrow she would turn to her affairs and meet with the sculptor.

He would pay her in cash – maybe even smile while he was doing it.

Her path was now downhill and the dark sea was in full view under the moon. There was the thinnest sliver of light above the hills across the firth. Like a lever opening the sky. And then she heard a startling sound. A bird began to sing. She didn't know what kind of a bird it was, but its sound was long and loud. It was answered by another. And another. A sequence of songs. A horse and wagon with rubber tyres clopped past in the direction of the city centre. And by the time it had gone, the dawn chorus was in full swing.

The time had come for her to sleep. She knew the milk she had heated earlier would have a skin on it. Nothing worse. She'd just have her biscuit while she was waiting for the water to boil for her jar. She'd curl around it and know that she would be asleep before she realised. Even the image of the dead man with the white pancake on his face would not prevent her from sleeping. She would insist that the sculptor would also pay the shivering boy for his journeys in the middle of the night. Such people should not be forgotten. The possibility existed that the sculptor would even praise the work she had done for him. That almost would be payment enough. And if he was scant with either his praise or payment, she had the consolation of the second impression beneath the towels in her hot press, which would, in its time, be a sort of pension for her old age.

THE FAIRLY GOOD

SAMARITAN

In his tiny one-roomed council flat, mostly in the mornings before going out, he likes to play Patience with a pack of cards which is so swollen with use that, when he handles a new deck in the pub, he thinks at least half of them are missing. He cheats only occasionally. When he does win honestly, for some reason, he feels disappointed. That's the worst thing.

After his breakfast he almost always forgets to wipe the table. That's why the cards end up the way they do. He deals and finds that one of them is missing. He looks beneath the table – under the bed – then finds the missing one in his hands, stuck precisely to its neighbour with jam.

'Cheap bloody rubbish.'

The more expensive playing cards, the ones with the lacquer finish, can be rubbed with a damp cloth and restored almost to their original freshness, so that they slide easily off one another. He likes jam. He can make a pot of blackcurrant last him three months, provided he spreads it thinly.

'On both bread and cards alike.'

This morning, descending the tenement stair aware of the sound of his stick, he notices Mrs Downstairs' door slightly ajar. She never leaves it that way, living as she does in terror of muggers and marauders. Or those, like himself, inclined to overdo the alcohol. She even closes it in the faces of various tradesmen and delivery people while she goes off down her hall to fetch their money. Once, she told him, she had had a coat, not worth very much – her shopping coat as opposed to her church-on-Sunday coat – stolen from her hallstand and the caller was nowhere to be seen. For ever afterwards, she was wary. And again one time in the street he saw her walk an evasive arc to circumnavigate a group of three Romanian women.

Because he has lost so many front-door keys, he keeps his own hidden at the back of the door on a piece of string long enough to be pulled out through the letter box. If any burglar discovers this ruse and is of a mind to, he can rifle him of his bit of cheese, his jam, his Bakelite radio. Even his deck of cards.

Apart from Mrs Downstairs' open door, everything else is as usual. In the pub, sitting on the stool he always uses, he has his first drink of the day. It tastes okay – but he doesn't drink because he likes the taste, he drinks because of what it does for him. It makes him feel better. The hand not steady but not shaking, either. He had once seen a man wearing a white silk scarf wrap one end of it around his glass hand and pull the other so that the drink came to his lips, as if on a pulley system. Not a drop did he spill. Things are not so bad if there's somebody worse . . .

For instance, the woman downstairs – the one whose door he had noticed open – she was a complete pain in the neck. It's as much as he can do to listen to her politely for the two or three minutes it takes her to deliver her charity. 'Well, how are we today?' and 'Would you like me to give you a haircut and trim that haystack of a beard?' or 'You haven't been feeding yourself properly.' She was from Lewis and had not lost an ounce of her accent.

If he buys three bottles of the cheapest-of-the-cheap and dilutes them a bit from the tap – not too much, mind you – he can get seven half bottles that'll last him the week. Throughout the day the longer he can put off drinking the half bottle, the more relaxed he is, the more he can look forward to the sitting before bed. And two pints a day to have on the marble counter in front of him in the pub. That's basic ration. After that, a glass here and a glass there bought by the odd stranger does not go amiss. Certain times of the year are better than others. An influx of tourists is always a good thing.

When Mrs Downstairs makes a pot of soup she always brings him up a bowl. If he is not there, she lets herself in with the key on the string and leaves the soup for him to reheat. Sometimes she'll leave him some potatoes that have gone blue-black with sitting, 'to fry up'. The woman thinks herself a saint. The only thing she never gives him is the thing he wants most. Money.

'I know you, you'd only spend it in the pub.'

Of course. What the fuck does she think he'd do with it. Buy new vests?

'The only booze I'd ever have in the house,' she said, 'is a half bottle of brandy. In case of illness.'

He hated that word – booze. It said so much about her. A word straight from the pulpit. Undiluted. What he cannot forgive her is her continual *interference*. An attribute of most saints.

'You need somebody to help you mend your ways, m'boy.'

'I'm much too old to change now.'

'It matters not how crooked the hook, the picture can always be hung straight.'

That's the kind of crap she comes out with all the time. Wee sayings. When the lecturing starts, he always nods his head and stares vaguely in the direction of the window.

This, she imagines, is her words sinking in. She always adds, in that silence, 'If you go on the way you're going, you'll kill yourself.'

And what, may I ask, do you think I'm trying to do? That is what he would like to say, but instead he maintains his stare in the direction of the window and continues the consoled nodding of his head. Soon, he thinks. If I was dead, look at the money I'd save. Neighbours are a good thing, provided they don't live too close.

The last time he was at the clinic for his winter flu jab the doctor had asked him how much he was drinking, and he told him the expected lie. He could see the doctor calculating the true figure.

'You're on a plateau,' he said, 'but I'd much prefer you to be off it altogether.'

'The drink or the plateau?'

But the doctor didn't laugh – he has the most wonderful deathbed manner – one of the mournfullest bastards on God's earth, looking over his half glasses and moving his pen arse-over-tip, pretending he knows what to say. It was a good consultation if he didn't recommend going in somewhere to dry out. And if he did?

'I do not allow myself even to think of those places, Doctor. Not again. Not ever.' He had, of his own accord, decided to give up many, many times. When he had money, he could drink as much as he wanted. Then came the warnings. He decided to monitor his intake by writing the date on the label. After a week he thought it more sensible to write the time of day. All that was long ago when he still had a certain amount of willpower and idealism. He had decided now to coast as pleasantly as possible to his end. He keeps himself as clean as his circumstances permit. But there are certain things outside his control. For instance, he imagines his feet smell and he tends to stay as far away from them as possible. This is difficult when sitting on a bar stool. Hot air rises. In the street this distancing between feet and nose results in a strange gait, which children mimic. Then they shake an imaginary stick in the air. It's the shoes that are at fault. Over the years they accumulate odours and their interiors, so far as he is aware, cannot be washed. He knows a few people who have more than one pair of shoes – but they are all women.

Mrs Downstairs runs a club. He bought his last pair of shoes from her catalogue and she made him pay them off at so much a week. She leaves the catalogue with him and he looks at the ladies' underwear section, remembering how it was. His glasses were of little help. He had found them glinting on a corporation dump. He would say, 'There's nothing wrong with my eyesight. It's just that there's not much of it.'

When he was ordering the shoes he told Mrs Downstairs of his reservations about his feet. She suggested he buy insoles – which absorb 'unwanted' smells. In their bought state they would fit a policeman, but the manufacturers have drawn dotted outlines around their peripheries so that the things may be cut to the required shoe size. He had not owned a pair of scissors since the early sixties and had to borrow a pair from herself.

Most days she brings him up yesterday's newspaper and he thanks her politely. If she neglects to call on him for several days, she has the required back-numbers with her. If there is one thing worse than a newspaper, it's a bundle of them. Then, when she is in the notion to tidy his place, she takes them all away again. He rarely opens them. He doesn't even use them to light the fire, because to light the fire you have to have something combustible, like coal, to put on top. Once he plaited paper sticks for her, and she was so delighted and went on about it so much that he never did it again. She reminds him of his great-aunt, the woman who reared him. Both his parents died in the same year when he was small, and Aunt Joyce felt obliged to take him over. Her whole life centred around manners.

'We must be *seen* to do the correct thing.' She had the ability to talk for hours without him registering a single word of what she was saying. It was during one such conversation, when he was eighteen, that he decided to disappear, finally. Mrs Downstairs seems to have modelled herself on all Aunt Joyce's principles. Right down to wearing the same navy hat when she went to church on Sundays. He'd often wondered, *could* it be the same one? Bought from a jumble sale to which Aunt Joyce had charitably contributed the contents of her wardrobe? Even though they lived a hundred miles and a generation apart?

He spent most days in the pub, with a break to see tour buses coming into the car park during the afternoon. He could see them arrive without even turning his head – in the mirror behind the bar. But the exercise was good for him. To stretch his legs. To watch the disgorging of visitors. In the distance the criss-cross of dockside cranes, the air coming off the sea tasting of ozone, clearing his head. One or two from the tour buses would come into the bar and he would retake his stool and initiate conversations with them. 'Social pole-vaulting' he called it. 'A flash of wit here, a pithy aphorism there.' In the course of most summer evenings there was a sufficiency of drink bought for him.

Now, this evening, on his way home he had had more than his fair share. He stopped more frequently than usual and leaned against various walls he knew. One of them was opposite his own tenement. He saw that the light was on in Mrs Downstairs' place and her curtains were still not pulled. The woman usually went to bed after the evening news on television. He tackled the stairs. Despite him calling her Mrs Downstairs, she lived on the first floor. All that mattered for his nickname to work was that she lived downstairs *from him*. Between pulling at the banisters and poling himself upwards with his stick, he made it to the first landing. He saw that her door was still ajar. He knocked with the bone handle of his stick but there was no response. He pushed the door but it was jammed. There was just enough of a gap for him to get his head in. Mrs Downstairs was lying behind the door blocking the way. She was wearing an overcoat and had an empty shopping bag looped over one arm.

He pushed her back with little shoulder-shoves of the door, so as not to hurt her, and got into the hallway. She now lay between the hallstand and the door. He lifted her hand. She was cold but not dead, because she tried to pull away from him. In her other hand she had a bottle of Nurse Harvey's Gripe Mixture and it had spilled all over her and she was sticky to the touch. It was even in her hair.

He went through to the bathroom and soaked a facecloth. The water was cold. No matter how long he ran it. There was a bathroom cupboard to one side of the wash-handbasin and he opened it with a wet finger. Medicines at the back of the shelf, old cough bottles, Dettol, eye-drops with black teat squeezers. Brown containers of tablets. A blue glass bottle of Milk of Magnesia. Flu remedies, Elastoplasts, plastic shower caps, cotton-wool pads, nail clippers, a pale-green-handled toothbrush in its packet, unopened. And there, right at the back, its shoulders standing clear of the ruck, the half bottle of brandy. He draped the wet facecloth over the rim of the sink and lifted the bottle by the neck to see the label. *Napoleon Brandy. Three years old.* He narrowed his eyes and tilted the label to the light. *Aged in oak casks, mellow and smooth, imported from France.*

'*Mais oui. Mais oui.*' He lifted the bottle clear of the cupboard and found it satisfyingly unopened. The meniscus was at the highest point in the bottle neck. He tilted it and the liquid gave a pleasant clink. He snapped the screw-cap and it clicked open. There was a little shearing noise as he unscrewed it.

'To the teetotaller, a bottle and a half bottle are the same thing.' Then he spoke out into the hallway. 'Thank you. I don't mind if I do.' A good swig, clenching hard, and after he had swallowed, 'Ya beauty.' With great care he set the bottle on the edge of the bath, then wrung out the facecloth. The wringings dribbled into the bath. He went back to the woman.

'Come on, dear.' He pulled her by the feet into the sitting room. She was wearing those opaque brown lisle stockings. She was some weight, and it took it out of him. He puffed and panted with the exertion. Her head gave a little nod as it passed over the raised threshold. Her eyes seemed to move as he pulled her closer to the centre of the room. As he lowered himself onto his knees he groaned loudly. With the facecloth he tried to clean the woman a bit, reduce the stickiness. He tugged her skirt down to make her decent.

'What are you like? Some strategy required here.' He left the facecloth on her shoulder and levered himself to a standing position. He went for the brandy. There was a tumbler on the draining board and he poured himself a substantial glass and drank from it. Much more civilised than necking the bottle. Glass and bottle were carried back into the room, where he set all on the coffee table. He felt the brandy doing him good. It added zest to everything. He sank into the armchair.

'You keep this great stuff in the cupboard for years on end, just hoping somebody'd become ill. Then, when the time comes . . . ' He raised the glass in her direction before drinking. 'Our healths,' he said. 'Speaking of which . . . '

He had not used a telephone for some years and felt uneasy lifting the receiver. He drank to steady himself, to give himself a bit of confidence.

'Which service do you require?'

'There is a woman very sick here. Stretched out, she is . . . at my feet.'

'Which service do you require? Fire, police or ambulance?'

'Ambulance, I think.'

'What is your number?'

'I don't know. You see, it's not my phone.'

'You need to speak up, sir, I cannot make out what you are saying.'

'It's not my fucking phone to know the number,' he shouted.

'It should be written on the dial, sir.'

'Forgive me, I can ill afford the luxury of bespoke spectacles. But I haven't got my stopgap pair at the moment.'

'Pardon?'

'I can't see very well.'

Anyway he got the business done and felt quite proud of himself. He turned his attention again to the patient. She was too heavy to lift and, besides, somewhere in the back of his head was the idea that he could do her some damage if she'd already broken something. Leave well enough alone. There was a tartan travelling rug on the sofa and he put that over her, after removing the wet facecloth from her shoulder.

'Don't worry. I've sent for an expert, my dear. He'll not be long now.'

The woman at his feet stirred and moaned a bit.

'It'll be all right. They'll not be long now.' He sat down again. Stretched his hands out to rest on the arms of the chair. He wondered what else he could do for her. He felt quite helpless just sitting there with his stick between his feet. Everything in the flat was as neat as ninepence. Her ornaments on the mantelpiece, her china cabinet, her two or three books, one of which was a fat Bible.

'Maybe a drop of this would do you good.' He started to laugh. 'Revive your spirits.' He leaned over and looked closely at her face. Her mouth was a little twisted but more closed than open. 'Don't want to waste anything.'

In getting to his feet, he created a momentum and charged ramstam against the wall. He held onto the radiator and steadied himself. Then to the bathroom. He held onto the handle of the bathroom door until he relocated the medicine cupboard. Then, in an attempt to open it, he fell – he didn't fall down completely but toppled over and grabbed a towel rail, which broke away from its moorings on the wall.

'Christ only knows what's happening here.' He started laughing. He was in a really good mood.

He got to his feet and selected a bottle of eye-drops. He unscrewed the eye-dropper and sluiced it out beneath the tap, then went back into the room.

'Can't have you poisoned.'

He opened and tilted the brandy bottle. The glass dropper filled and emptied as he squeezed and released its little black rubber bulb.

'Hold on there.' He got down on his knees and tried to insert the point of the dropper into the side of her mouth, which was open. He squeezed the bulb.

'Cheers,' he said. He realised he had not got a drink in his hand, so he leaned over to where his glass was and saluted her and drank. He refilled his glass. Beneath him the woman began to cough and wheeze. There was something wrong with her breathing. He got to his feet and made it to the kitchen sink. He poured a little water into a cup and brought it to her.

'Here.' He took her head and raised it up a little and touched the cup to her lips. Her lips had gone even more askew, in fact the whole left side of her face seemed to have slipped. The water just dribbled down the side of her cheek.

Suddenly the woman let a groan out of her, and again he reassured her help would be along in a minute. The grey hair beside her neck was all stuck to her face with the Gripe Mixture and she seemed to be getting a worse colour – a leathery yellow. Then she made another noise – a kind of bubbling in her throat. He got off the sofa and turned her head to the side. She was sick a little out of the downside of her mouth. He slipped a newspaper under the side of her head to save the carpet.

'You're in a right fucking mess now, eh? Shall I call a minister?'

She lay inert, her head cradled in the newspaper.

Then he heard an ambulance in the distance. It came closer and closer, then stopped, the blue light flashing up into the room on the ceiling. It was probably the only night in her life when she hadn't pulled the curtains. Feet sounded on the stairs and two ambulance people came in, finding the door open. They were dressed in green boiler suits.

'The Irish team have arrived,' he said. He was sure one of them was a woman. He hadn't expected that. They did what they had to do with the patient, fumbling in their holdalls, squirting syringes into the air, speaking quietly to one another. Then the ambulance man said he was going off for a stretcher. The other one, who was still kneeling, asked, 'What's the name?' It was a woman's voice.

'Her name?'

'Yes.'

'Eh . . . I . . . think, it's Maudey.' The ambulance woman leaned down and used the woman's name over and over again. 'Everything is going to be all right, Maudey.'

'I forget her second name. I just call her Mrs Downstairs.'

'You're not related then?'

'Good God, no. I'm the occupant from above.'

'Oh, you're the good Samaritan who phoned . . . '

'Fairly good,' he said. 'Thanks, but there's no need to mention it.'

'Does she live on her own?'

'As far as I know. She musta felt poorly when she was going out. Thus the gripe water. The shopping bag.'

The ambulance woman went about her business, looking here and there, going out to the door and writing some details in a small notebook. She came back in.

'Do you have a key for this place?' she said.

'No, I don't. The door was open.'

'We have to secure the premises.'

The ambulance woman looked in the shopping bag. A purse. A jingle of keys. The ambulance woman disappeared and there was a noise as she tried the various keys in the lock. She came back into the room and said, 'Right' in a very determined way. The first ambulance man arrived back with a stretcher. It was more a folding trolley than anything else. They manoeuvred Mrs Downstairs onto it and bustled out with her – one of them at either end. The trolley clanged as they guided it down the stairs.

He continued to sit on the sofa for some time with the remains of the half bottle. He thought about leaving a little for Mrs Manners, but in the end decided not to. He didn't like stealing – although in some way he felt he'd earned it. More like sharing her hospitality. He set the empty bottle neatly in a wastepaper basket by the hearth. There was stuff in the basket. Scrunched-up paper, bits of orange peel, a scramble of grey hair. With the tip of his stick he moved some of the discarded paper, but there was nothing of any interest lower down.

The ambulance woman came in again. This time she was panting. She said, 'It's lights-out time.'

'Pardon?'

'It's goodnight. We have to secure the premises.' She helped him out of the sofa. For a woman, she had a stiff strong arm. There was a whiff of disinfectant about her. He stood wavering, before he set his glass on the draining board.

'And may flights of angels guide thee to thy rest.'

'You're upstairs?' she said.

'Indeed I am.'

She held onto his arm and guided him to the door.

'Just a minute.' She propped him behind the front door and went back into the room and took one last look around, before unplugging the TV and switching off the lights. Then the hall lights. Then she slammed the door behind them. The noise echoed round the stairwell, which was continually flashing blue and black.

'Will you be all right?'

'Some day soon.'

His hand on the banisters steadies him. He hauls with one hand while he puts all his weight on his stick with the other. The brass ferrule clicks against the stone steps.

'Goodnight, sir,' she says.

'Goodnight, my dear,' he says.

A jingling sound of keys comes from the ambulance woman as she dances her way down to street level.

THE END OF DAYS

Vienna 1918

He had never seen the like of it before. Coming from the bathroom, he stopped in the hallway. The place was dark and silent and there was a chill in the air. What drew his attention was low on the skirting board – about the size of a *korona* or a small silver coin, perfectly bright. Incandescent even. What could it be? There seemed to be no origin for it. He bent his knee and went down close. He put his hand out in front of him at ankle level and the brightness appeared on the back of his hand. Then he moved his hand so that the light was always on it. Was it a reflection from something bright? He had to get up from his semi-kneeling position and was drawn towards the studio door, still with the disc of light balancing on the tendons of his hand. Then he saw the source. The light was coming from the keyhole. How amazing. He swung the door open and the room beyond was drenched with the brightest of bright sunlight. Doubled, if anything, by the full-length mirror. He could see the dust on the glass of the windows – it had the delicacy of fine lace, but he could not look at the October sun itself. He would tell her about this little epiphany. It might cheer her.

He stopped at the bedroom where she was now sleeping and listened. There was no sound. The door was not firmly shut and the light was subdued by the shutters he had partially closed the night before. She did not like complete darkness. Made her afraid, she said. He put his head around the door. Her tousled hair on the pillow, the bed-clothes accumulated around her in heaps, a bare foot at the bottom of the bed.

The kitchen was ice-cold. He looked out at the roofs. There was still some frost to be seen in the shadows of the chimneys of the primary school. The sun, up earlier than him, had reduced most of the whiteness to wet black slates.

He raked the stove, filling the air with a film of ash and dust. He was aware of it on his tongue. Mouth breathing. There were still some viable cinders and these he set aside to help light the fire. The war had affected everything. The only coal they got, if they could lay hands on any at all, left a residue of slate and rocks. It did not burn away but clogged the firebox with laminates of chalk, bits of stone. He checked the coal scuttle. It was empty except for a few fragments in black dust. The same way the flour bin was empty except for white dust. Shortages of the black and the white. Why should he have to do all this? He went out the back door into the yard and emptied the ash pan into the bin. There was just enough wind to swirl the dust up into his face and it came so quickly that he had not time to avert his face. To turn the other cheek, as it were. He choked and spat a little into the drain. Spitting at home, he felt, was permissible. He went to the coalhouse and scraped together whatever was left. Slack. A month ago it had been a small heap of coal. It was all he could get. There was no lack of money – he had never been so well off – but you just could not buy what you wanted.

He still had some newspaper pages and these he crushed and put into the firebox and covered with kindling. Then the cinders, then the coal fragments. He lit the newspaper and let the sticks catch. Then gradually increased the draught.

He'd chopped the sticks with an axe outside in the yard at the weekend. The exercise had helped him get rid of some of his anger. It was just after Lucille, their maid, had walked out on them. It was understandable, because she was afraid. Everyone was afraid. She had gone home to the country – the place where most people wanted to be at a time like this. If you were deeply afraid, that is. Somehow your own family seemed like the only people in the world who would not have the sickness.

He knew his wife had chosen Lucille for her looks. Or lack of them. The maid was much too heavy, pudgy – always blowing and puffing when she had work to do – her face jowled and her left eye turned in a little, looking towards her nose. She had only been working for them since the summer.

It took a long time to boil the kettle. Then he boiled one of the remaining eggs for four minutes. His wife Edi had managed to get them from a friend who kept her own chickens. If Edi wouldn't eat the egg, he would. He put out the last bread roll for her – it was stale enough to hear it hit against the plate. Closer to a biscuit than to bread. He considered sawing it in two with the bread-knife, but the resultant crumbling would be a waste. If she wanted smaller pieces it would be easier to break it with her hands. Or soften it in her tea. But unless you baked it yourself these days, bread was very difficult to come by. It was Edi, herself, who normally did the baking, with Lucille looking on. There was a warp on the tray so that things were wont to sit slightly unsure of themselves.

On his way to her bedroom he kept his eye off the tray. To focus on his destination increased the surety of his balance and steadied whatever it was he was carrying. He pushed the door open with his foot and set the tray on the dressing table.

'Edi,' he said softly. Then more loudly, until the noise of her breathing was interrupted. She made some muffled reply. He opened the shutters a little more, enough to let sufficient light in, but not so much as would create a glare for someone just waking. He then helped her up into a sitting position, turned and plumped her pillows so that they made a back for her against the bedhead. He turned and rested the tray on her lap as best he could.

'Well, how do you feel?' She gazed down at the tray, stupefied. She did not answer – which was an answer in itself.

'You must eat something,' he said. 'Keep up your strength.'

She reached out for the glass of water and drank it – almost in its entirety. She paused a little to get breath, before raising the glass perpendicularly to empty it. She gasped loudly. To swallow *and* breathe was difficult.

'Not hungry?'

She shook her head while making a little sneer with the side of her mouth. He told her about the spot of light he had found on the back of his hand earlier, which he mistook at first for a silver coin. But he might as well be speaking a foreign language for all the interest she took. Eventually she said, 'What time is it?'

'Just after ten.'

'The school. I don't hear the children.'

'They have very strict teachers,' he smiled, 'to keep them quiet.'

'It's break time. When they scream their heads off. In the playground. Their teachers are elsewhere.'

'I read somewhere they were thinking of closing the schools. If things got worse.'

'That'll be it,' she said. 'Things must've got worse.'

'Don't be so negative.'

She reached out and her hand hovered over the bread roll but she did not take it. Her hand was shaking as she reached for the teapot.

'I find it hard to imagine a child of ours at that school anyway.'

He intervened and poured the tea for her. A little steam rose from the cup.

'This is a treat,' he said. 'The shakings of the tea caddy.'

She picked up the cup and blew on the surface of the tea. Then set it down again without drinking.

'I'm frightened,' she said. Her voice was only just audible. On the verge of tears.

'What?'

'Many people die from it.'

'From going to school?'

'No.' She knew he was being obtuse to amuse her. 'From this.' She pointed at herself, at her being an invalid. 'Lucille said that a healthy man at breakfast could be dead by teatime.'

'Lucille. Who'd listen to Lucille? Many, many people don't die from it. The majority recover.' He sounded as if he was the voice of reason.

He sat down on the bed beside her and put his arm around her. She rested her head on his shoulder. He felt the heat rising from her face to his cheek. Like a brazier. He drew back and looked at her. The glass of water had gone through her almost immediately and was coming out in beads on her forehead. And her upper lip. She picked up her cup and sipped the tea, after again blowing on it. Still he held onto her. Lightly tapped her stomach with his long fingers.

'Feels like a drum,' he said. 'Is it still busy?' He caressed her through her nightclothes.

'He's still exercising. Occasionally.'

'Maybe her. Your belly button sticks out – more and more.'

'I can't help that. It's the way it is.'

Then, in response to his tapping, he felt a ripple beneath his hand. A definite movement.

'I feel it,' he said. 'It's a kind of tongue in cheek. If you'll excuse the expression.'

'Whatever it is, I just wish it would take a rest. Might be distressed because of me being sick.'

'You should rest,' he said and kissed her on the forehead. 'Then maybe it will calm down.' She fended him off with her arm.

'You will get it from me,' she said. He helped her lie flat again, drew the bedclothes around her body. Tucked her in. Like his mother did for him when he was young. Edi closed her eyes.

'I was amazed the first time I ever saw a pregnant woman,' he said. 'I was with my mother on the street. Did I tell you this?'

She shook her head. She lifted a corner of the sheet and wiped her mouth, then the rest of her face.

'I thought the woman was trying to hide something. Maybe something she'd stolen. And I asked Mama, "Why does that woman have a basin up her coat?" Of course Mother was embarrassed. But she gave me a straight answer. That didn't often happen in those days. Her motto was to keep us ignorant. Ignorance is innocence. She said, "She's going to have a baby." I think that confused me even more.'

Back in the kitchen, he scoured the inside of the shell with the spoon. The egg white came away in the contour of the shell. He wolfed it. By now it was cold. He ate the stale bread. It sounded like toast.

Some days before Edi took to her bed, they had stopped in town for a coffee in one of the best of places. A mid-afternoon celebration they had promised themselves since his contribution to the exhibition had sold out. He was never sensible with money and this place could serve delights, war or no war. They could get milk, they could

111

get cream, even chocolate. But at a price. The waiter arrived with their order. The tables were crowded, despite the authority's restrictions. Edi was facing the door, he had his back to it. Lifting the coffee cup to her face, she sipped and smiled. 'I've only seen one playwright,' she said.

'And one philosopher.'

'Who? Who is the philosopher?'

'His name wouldn't mean anything to you,' he said with a smile.

She pulled a face in retaliation, stuck her tongue out a little.

'Behave,' he said. 'Being married to the likes of you is supposed to improve *me*.'

As if to demonstrate, she lifted her pastry fork to slice a portion of her torte, but stopped. Her eyes stared over his shoulder. 'What's this?' she said.

'What?' He turned and followed her gaze.

'He's drunk.'

A well-dressed middle-aged man was approaching unsteadily. He stopped to look for an empty table. His face was a bad colour. Then he put out his hand to one side as if to steady himself. Other people began to notice him, to raise eyebrows. A waiter in full-length white apron spotted him and made to intervene. Then the man lurched forward and to one side and fell against the sweet trolley with a crash, scattering everything onto the floor. A plate broke and bits of it slid in among everyone's feet, in between the table and chair legs. Cream cakes were upended, as were tartlets and a plate of Viennese whirls. There was a crowd reaction – somewhere between an intake of breath and 'How dare they allow such people to enter!' Some leapt to their feet, a woman wiped her mouth with her napkin. The man who had fallen lolled his head back then turned to the side and blood began to well up from his mouth and cascade onto the wooden floor.

'Jesus!'

'Ooh no.'

'The fool . . . '

'What a terrible mess.'

The noise the man was making was half choking, half vomiting. The lower half of the waiter's full-length apron was instantly spattered with red. Edi didn't know whether to cover her eyes or her ears. In horror, she brought her gloved hands to her mouth and stood. The broken crockery was still spinning and moving around her pale shoes. All the waiters now came running, alerted by the noise. Edi did not even have to say anything. Her look was enough. Let's get out of here. But, between blood and overturned pastries, the way to the door was impassable. She looked around frantically for an alternative. A rotating side door was already in use, gulping coffee-smelling air and expelling it onto the street as customers pushed and elbowed one another to leave. Edi led the way, tiptoeing to the exit as quickly and as gracefully as she could. Outside, she noticed for the first time a tram conductor wearing a white face mask and then she realised what had just happened.

He tried her again with food in the afternoon. But with no success. When he lifted her up onto her pillows, he felt her tremble. Her very frame was in vibration with the effort. She refused food, but drank more water. This time he sat in a bedside chair, staring at her.

'What am I going to do with you?'

'Every bone in my body aches,' she said. But she spoke so quietly he had to lean forward and she repeated herself. Then said, 'I've definitely got it.'

'It's ordinary influenza. You'll be up by the end of the week.'

She stared at him. He looked back. Saw everything.

'Can I draw you?' he said. She seemed unsure. 'Just your head and shoulders?'

'As long as I don't have to do anything,' she said.

He got up and fetched his sketchbook and crayons from the studio. She had not the energy to worm herself back beneath the bedclothes, so was still sitting up the way he left her. He sat down on the bedside chair and turned to a fresh but yellowing page, crossed his legs and leaned the book against his knee.

He began the process of looking. Up at her, down at the page. Again and again, like a bird drinking. His hand motioning but not drawing. Not contacting the paper with the crayon. The way a singer would try phantom notes before going onstage, making sure that he still had a voice.

And he began.

'Can you bear to lift your hand up to your face?'

She did what she was asked. Her arm moved, her index finger took its rest somewhere between her cheekbone and her ear. She was as practised at being drawn as he was at drawing.

'Can you close your mouth?'

114

She obeyed. She is burning. Smouldering – not lit from the window, but from inside. Looking and sweeping his crayon, looking and outlining. Black on cream. Sometimes the line is like the human voice. It sings. Variations and complexities. And the line gives back, just as the voice does. It reveals. Volume as loudness. Volume as bulk. Even the emptiness on the page is part of the voice. The tumbling of her hair in a topknot, catching her likeness, looking and narrowing his eyes to draw her eyes, heavily lidded with sickness. Adding a ring to her finger, looking and opening a line for the emptiness of her hanging sleeve. Her hair like smoke rising from the fire of her raging fever.

The way he looked up at her when he'd finished was a different kind of looking.

'Let me see,' she said. He handed her the book.

She looked at the drawing and sighed, '"The Wreck of the Hesperus".' She handed it back and he signed the logo of his name at the bottom left-hand corner. Then dated it.

'You're becoming so fast,' she said. 'It feels like I haven't had time to breathe.'

He got up and began to tidy away his crayons. Edi tried to say something else, but instead of words she began a seemingly endless fit of coughing into her handkerchief. It happened again and again. Every time she attempted to say something, she exploded into coughing. Then she reached out and silently beseeched paper from him. Took a crayon from his paraphernalia. Tore away half a page, leaned the page fragment on the pad against her raised knees and wrote in her spidery hand. That she loved him.

He nodded, understanding. But she shook her head as if he had not understood. She took back the paper and, still holding her handkerchief to her mouth, wrote with her other hand that her love was without limit, beyond measurement. Until the end of time.

He went to the studio and set down his materials on the desk. For a long time he stood in front of the full-length mirror, his gaze drifting from his reflected face to his reflected hands. Self-regarding. He repositioned his hands, parted his fingers and considered the reflection. Curious, but an improvement. It was too cold for this. He turned his back on the mirror, picked up his writing paper and sat into his desk. He really should warn his mother. And while he was at it, tell her that she was due to become a grandmother by Christmas. A pen with a favourite nib was what he was looking for. Before he began he covered his shoulders with a blanket. He opened the ink bottle and dipped. Dear Mother, he wrote, in his neat, almost perfect handwriting. He told her that Edith had contracted Spanish flu some days ago and that it had become pneumonia. He thought the form of it was serious and life-threatening. Also that she was now six months pregnant and that he was preparing himself for the worst. He used the rocker blotter to make sure the ink was dry before folding the paper. Even then he didn't trust it, but had to blow a little stream of air over the page.

He stopped for a while outside Edi's bedroom and listened but could hear nothing. With his heavy dark overcoat, a woollen scarf that doubled as a face mask and his hat, he was ready to go. He slipped the letter into his coat pocket. The postbox was nearby and he could call at the shop at the corner to see if any fresh bread had come in. Or if they had anything else that was fresh.

At that time of afternoon there were very few about. Everybody seemed to be hunkering down and waiting until the awfulness passed. The leaves of most trees had fallen, but some still clung on. He loved autumn better than any other season but somehow not this particular autumn. There was also fruit hanging from the branches but he had no names for them. Some were like grey lamb's tails, others were round and black against the sky, like nuts. Here and there a few red haws were left by the birds. He posted his letter and imagined his mother opening it. She would cry, of that there was no doubt. She always whined – about everything. 'Why don't you get yourself a job in the railway?' His boyhood was trains – the sound of them, the sight of them. He woke and fell asleep to them clattering through the station where they lived. At home he played with model trains, constantly drew trains. 'Your father made a good living at it. He was a respected man.' When he was stationmaster at Tulln, his father wore a uniform. Hanging by his side on special occasions, a sword. They buried him in this uniform. At the end he was almost blind and didn't know what day of the week it was. It was years afterwards that he found out that his father died of syphilis.

The air was chilled and the sky, a featureless slate-grey, was waiting to rain. There was nothing fresh in the shops. It was hardly worth going out of his way to the coal yard. The last time he had passed it, a workman had been brushing the concrete clean. A ghostly sound, like harsh, intermittent breathing.

On his way home he crossed a wooded shortcut he knew. A mist was building up. A miasma. Looking around him, he saw some dead branches, and as he was picking up the kindling, he noticed the remains of a door. It was hidden in an undergrowth of fallen leaves, dead grasses and stiffened cow parsley and it took him some time to free it. It was only the lower half of a door, rotting away. Whoever had dumped it had removed any metal from it – the letter box, the door handle, what his father-in-law referred to as door furniture – and this process had left yawning holes. He discarded the kindling he had gathered and tugged the door free. He could carry it clear of the ground. If it began to feel heavy he could trail it behind him. Why should he be scavenging like this, with his wallet full of money? It had taken longer than he thought to free the door and now the light was fading. Was it night? Or storm darkness? Or a combination of the two? It would cloak any shame he had in trailing his booty. He left the shortcut and was into streets again. Before the next corner a voice called to him.

'Like to pass some time with me, soldier?'

He looked up. A girl, difficult in the light to tell what age she was. She stood in a doorway, one foot flat against the upright. Her pale thigh horizontal and jutting from her slit skirts. Advertising. He stopped, tried to see what she looked like. There were several steps, dished with wear, which led up to the entrance. He rested his ridiculous half door-frame against a railing and climbed to be on a level with her. She was attractive but looked none too clean. He was aware of his full wallet nudging at his heart. He loosened off the scarf around his mouth and nose. Let his guard fall.

'I don't have much time,' he said.

'Some guys don't take too long.'

He questioned her about what she would do, and for what price. There was a long pause as he considered. She thought he was going to haggle.

'I haven't seen you before,' he said.

'I've just come down from the north. Prague.' Hearing this, he raised his scarf around his mouth and nose. Tightened it. In these times everything was dangerous. There was another long pause and he began backing away from her. But he didn't lose sight of her dark eyes, her extruded thigh. What he said next was muffled.

'Maybe sometime again,' he said. 'Do you pose? Naked?'

'What?'

He repeated what he said a little louder.

'If it pays I'll do it,' she said.

'It's not as easy as you think. Keeping still.'

'Oh, I can keep still. Or I can give you two dunts for every one of yours – whatever you like, soldier. Or maybe you're not one of our battle-weary boys at all. What's this about posing? Are you an artist?'

'You might say that,' he smiled at her. 'But I'm fond of afters.'

'It's all included, if the price is right.'

'And I can find you here?'

'Here or hereabouts. If I'm not here, ask for Melita.'

He backed down the steps, still looking at her.

'Oh – d'you mind me asking? What age are you?'

'Eighteen.'

'If you believe that, you'll believe anything,' he said. *'She told me, Your Honour, that she was eighteen.'*

The girl laughed.

'Cheeky,' she said.

He waved, even though his back was now turned. He picked up his door fragment and continued to wave with his free hand.

As he walked away he heard a church bell start up. Then another began faintly in the distance. And another. They were like dogs barking in the countryside, starting one another off. The first bell was not the cathedral's. He knew the sound of it, the Old Pummerin, and had a fondness for it because – so he'd been told – it had been cast from 300 cannons. Anything was better than war. But he couldn't tell which particular church had started the present pealing. It was more like a death knell than anything else. He was far from his Catholic origins and he wondered what the occasion was.

It was night by the time he got home. From the street he could see her light faintly. He went to listen at Edi's door but heard only silence. Back in the kitchen, he began to chop the door fragment into pieces to fit the firebox. Some millipedes and slaters ran from the light when he hatcheted the rotting wood. He stamped them before they could get as far as the dark of the skirting boards. He set the fire for the morning. Left the matches where he would find them.

On his way to bed he called in to check if Edi wanted anything. She was still asleep. Her breath droned and fluttered. Seemed more intermittent and unsettled than it was in the afternoon. It was not the breathing of rest but a troubled sound, of squeaks and creaks like floorboards underfoot. He thought her a strange colour. More of an absence of colour. Like a black-and-white drawing. Maybe it was the poor quality of the light. Her lips seemed grey and there were other parts of her face discoloured.

'You poor thing,' he whispered. He left the light on, in case she would be afraid if she awakened.

He did not know why he woke. He lay still, waiting for some explanation. It was just after six and still dark. Then he heard a kind of howl. He tumbled out of bed and ran towards the sound. It went on and on. In her room he went to her and held her, shushing her constantly. 'Edi, poor Edi.' But still she continued to make the noise. He had pulled her into an upright sitting position, hoping it would help her breathing. He cradled her in his arms. She was shaking. Trembling but unaware of him. Her eyes were open but not seeing.

There was bright scarlet blood covering the white pillow. She was making the noise but could not get a breath, could not get under the breath to help push out more of the noise.

'Edi, Edi,' he said, trying to calm her. But she was not to be calmed. He clenched her in his arms, hoping to squeeze her into submission, to stop the gargling noises that were coming from her. Her eyes were looking towards the darkness of the partially shuttered window. It was as if he was rescuing her from drowning. Two people who could not swim in deep water – one who could breathe, the other who couldn't.

'I'll go for the doctor . . . ' he said. But he knew it was too late. Knew that if he left her and went out into the night, she would die on her own. With nobody to hold onto. So he stayed and closed his own eyes. Stroked her back. Clenched her to him. And the more he squeezed, the more she trembled. He did not know how long this went on for. It could have been a minute or ten minutes or half an hour, but gradually she quietened. The exhalation was all. No breath was being taken in to be turned around and given out again. Her blood was smeared on his shoulder. She stopped breathing. There was silence. He turned over the pillow and laid her head back down.

'Edith?'

He leaned close to her. Pulled down her lacy neck and put his right ear to her chest. Silence. 'Edi,' he said. 'Please.' He was looking up under her chin. His own voice reverberated back from her sternum. But nothing else. He tried to find her pulse, the one in her neck. But he either could not find it or it was not there. He pulled back from her. Her lips were purple. Again he pulled down the neck of her nightclothes and pressed his other ear to her chest. A churning noise. Was it the sound of her blood pulsing around her? Through her arteries and veins. Or was it the noise of the friction between her skin and the skin of his ear? A sandpaper sound. He steadied himself. Tried not to move in any way. There was something. A pulse was coming from somewhere. A faint drumming. Whatever it was, it seemed distant. He drew back and looked at her face. Her eyes were unseeing, turned to the ceiling. He returned his ear to her chest. Undeniably the sound was still there. Hollow. Faint. Far away. But there all the same. Like faint palpitations. A sound like the sound from his childhood – the beat of trains over tracks. Moving across a junction. Galloping. Remote. As he listened he was looking down her body towards her feet. Past the rise that was her stomach. And the realization of what he was hearing dawned upon him. It was not his wife's heartbeat, but that of his child. Now becoming faster and fainter with distress. His nameless child. He listened until it faltered and stopped. Stillness. He pulled away and covered his face with his knuckled hands.

He went to their own bedroom and stared out the dark window without seeing anything. Gradually light began to define the shapes outside. Trees, chimneys, roofs slowly declared themselves over time, out of the dawn. Birds began to sing and criss-cross the window. Most of the trees were now stripped bare of their leaves and beaded with rain. He began to cough and could find no way to stop coughing. When the bout finally did stop, he drank water. He had to rest for some time before he could move again.

For some reason he turned to her wardrobe and opened it. Dresses and blouses and camisoles. He recognised them all, from having drawn her countless times – could see each drawing again. Vertical candy-stripes, some black and white, some multicoloured. Modern outfits of silk and serge and voile. He could smell them without moving his face towards them – her various perfumes, eau de cologne, lavender water. He moved closer and got the basenote of her, what lay beneath the shop scent. That which exuded Edith. Her smell. He brushed across the hanging garments with the back of his hand and the sensation intensified. The clothes rippled in response. Wind over the ripeness of a summer field. But he missed the dresses of his grandmother's day, which trailed the floor as the wearer walked. Made a noise of sighing just behind her footstep.

Built into the wardrobe was a low chest of drawers. He opened one. A compartment for headbands, another for jewellery, yet another for hairpins and hair combs and kerchiefs. Lace collars and neck pieces. He went through the other drawers. One for belts and cummerbunds. One for automobile scarves, cravats and neckerchiefs. One for gloves, elbow-length and ordinary, *chamoisettes* – with or without buttons. Mitts and muffs. And at the bottom, compartments where he stooped to examine her white underthings. He returned all to the state he found them, with pressure from his knee. Above his head on a shelf, hats and hat boxes. Black fascinators, feathers, different-coloured chin straps, hats with brims broad enough to overhang the shelf. And at his feet, her polished boots and shoes. In pairs, heels facing outwards. The occasional individual shoe toppled sideways. Oxfords, pumps, snake-skins. And the white button-top boots she'd worn that awful day in the coffee shop. Since wiped clean of the spotting.

It was now clear daylight. He looked at his watch. Heard its chain rattle against the case as he replaced it in his pocket. They wouldn't be up yet. He took another fit of coughing. It sounded like a dog barking.

He wandered back into the room where Edi lay. He found it difficult to look at her. He just did not know how to behave. He felt he should cry – but he couldn't. What should he do? Should he listen again? The shutters had to be fully opened. When he had done that, he looked across the street but could see no sign of movement in the house opposite. His mother-in-law's place. Frau Harms would be devastated. And Edith's sister, Adele.

They would not begin to move for several hours yet. There seemed no point in wakening them with such heart-breaking news at this time of the morning. He opened the window a little to air the room.

This was where he had first seen Edith – across this canyon of a street. It had begun with a stare – then a shy disappearance. White. The way the scut of a rabbit is all that's remembered when it flees. The next day at the same time another stare, a little longer, led to an incline of the head. The day after that, she'd brought another girl – later he found out it was Adele – to show him off. He'd tried to amuse them with hand gestures that he had practised in front of the mirror. And, when he was within earshot, Indian whoops. They'd ended up laughing and smiling at him. He had walked across the street and introduced himself – much to Frau Harms' unease, a feeling that only increased, the more she learned about him. In the early days he had sought permission from her to take her daughters to see films at the Zentral Kino, if you don't mind, using his lover at the time, Wally, as a kind of gooseberry.

*

The draught from the window made him shiver. The air had an early-morning chill to it. He closed and locked the window. Then turned to the bed. Despite having had little or no sleep, he felt an urge to work. But the lack of sleep had given him a headache. And he began to feel feverish. In the past when he'd been ill with fever he'd felt a compulsion. To get things done. Work and fever were partners. Creativity rose with the mercury. A high temperature helped what went on paper. Then the illness took over. Defied what it had first encouraged. And the crayon dropped.

He raced to the studio and came back with his drawing materials.

'Forgive me,' he said. He pulled the bedclothes to the foot of the bed. Walked around the bed, looking. His eyes began to burn and he clenched them shut for a moment because he found he could focus better when he opened them. He did not want to move her. Or touch her. Her ankles and her toes. They seemed in shadow. Or were they just darker? Had her skin turned ebony-like? Her left hand was turned to the ceiling, with fingers slightly curled. Her right was clenched, the knuckles pale and shining. Her nostrils seemed to have enlarged. Changed shape, even. He hardly recognised her. Her nightclothes rumpled, pulled this way and that as she had burned with the fever. She was exposed in places. Accidentally. Self-consciously. Awkwardly. In an attempt to cool. He hurried from the room and came back with a set of library steps. He positioned the steps so as his back would be to the window. He climbed three treads and steadied himself at the top, his hand on the post. Then got his pad and crayon and began to draw, looking down from the height. The black and the white. How he loved it. The infallibility of his line. Laying it down so fast he heard his own breathing begin to race after a while, heard his weak heart quicken. He thought there was a first time for everything, but then he remembered earlier in the year drawing his friend and mentor, the dead Klimt, in the morgue after he had succumbed to the same disease. He made three drawings of the artist he admired most.

Edith was lard-white, slowly becoming grey. Her hair, which he thought of as smoke when he last drew her, now he saw as seaweed. Strands of stuff left on a beach by a high tide. Framing her head on the overturned pillow with yellow-brown and orange-red. Titian, some people called the colour. Edi's Titian hair. And the orb of her stomach, almost bursting through. Indeed, her skin could be seen where the material of her nightclothes had ridden up her body.

He almost toppled because he became so absorbed in what he was doing, he forgot where he was. On the top step. But steadied himself against the post with his drawing hand. Accuracy was what he was after. Accuracy and an intensity of awareness. Paying attention with his eyes. With the weight of his crayon as it unfurled its line. A flourish or two to finish. There. He stepped back down the treads and tore off the drawing and set it on the dressing table. Keep the momentum. He moved the steps to the foot of the bed and completed another drawing faster, if anything, than the first. This time with foreshortening. He was on fire. He set it on top of the first one on the dressing table. When he lifted the library steps to move them, he was aware of a tremor. Either it was the weight of the steps or his own weakness. Vibration. Shaking. A fluttering around his heart. This third drawing showed evidence of a shaking line from the crayon. And he loved the effect. The tremulousness of it. His headache from the sleeplessness was getting worse, but he ignored it. The pressure to capture overcame the pain. But he could not stop his teeth chattering. Where had this symptom come from? He was so cold. The next time he changed the position of the library steps, he pulled a blanket out from the bedclothes and draped it around his shoulders. That was better. But it did not last long. Again he became as cold as ice – even beneath the blanket. In this drawing Edi had no head. The rise of her shoulder and the angle he was seeing her from seemed to block it out. But no matter. It might work. Because the swell of her stomach was too important to ignore. And the sadness it contained. The shaking line encapsulating it was strong, sinewy. His shivering gave to the line what vibrato gives to a violin string. Plumped it up, adding richness and depth and mystery. Her body being both cradle and coffin, within a minute. He was frightened. Knew he was getting it too? Was it possible to die in tandem? He lost count of how many drawings he had made. But he felt instinctively they were good. How much better to draw women than fight wars.

But this was not what he should be doing. From his height he looked across the street. No sign of movement. The shaking that had taken over his body was now too much. There was a danger he would fall off the library stool. Could forget where he was and take a step backwards, to give his eye distance. And topple. He was reluctant to interrupt the outpouring of line – wanted to give the draughtsman in him total freedom. Seeing in and around the line. Seeing through the line to the creamy paper. Feeling the line engender such weight, such bulk. But his knees were shaking and it was dangerous. He completed the drawing and stepped backwards slowly down to the floor. The fire. He remembered setting the fire the night before. He was so cold. Another blanket. He tugged another one from the bed and draped it over his shoulders.

In the kitchen he found matches where he'd left them and lit the fire. He pulled a bentwood armchair close to the stove and sat, shaking and staring. The pale flames, edged with blue, moving up the crumpled newspapers. The door he'd dragged home and reduced to kindling wood had been painted and he watched it bubble as the fire engulfed it, cracking and spitting. The cinders glowed as they caught, the coal fragments reddened at the edges. He increased the draught. Felt heat coming in his direction. But it was of little use. It could not reach into his bones, which were cold at the centre of him. Each limb with its core of cold bone. Was this trying to tell him something? Edi with child, stretched on a bed. And him unable to weep? His only response, to draw her? Over and over again. What a fucking jerk he was. All the women of his life . . . He caught sight of himself briefly in the kitchen mirror – looked like an old shawlie. A woman in her eighties. Scared him a little, at first glance. Just one more woman to add to the queue of women. Edi had been a change, someone good. Someone respectable to be his wife. Carefully chosen to be advantageous. And she had carried out her strait-laced role so well. Three married years of enhancing him. Encouraging people's respect for him. Because to say that his reputation was in the gutter was to speak too highly of it. Certainly her mother, Frau Harms, fought tooth and nail to end the relationship with what she called 'This fly-by-night. This purveyor of pornography'. What airs and graces! In arguments with his wife, Egon would say, 'If my mother-in-law doesn't like it, I must be doing something right.' Other times, especially of late, Mother-in-law could be cordial enough. She and Egon had constructed a way of behaving and working, of falsely smiling while in each other's company. 'Nothing wrong with a little politeness,' was what she said. But Edi had fought her corner, insisted her man was good at heart and stuck by him. As for the father, old Johann, he was easier to handle. He was a locksmith who became a railway engineer. Egon even liked him. He became a substitute for his own dead father. And he used this fondness to gain Edi's respect. Be nice to the father and she would seek to repay the favour. Egon did many drawings and portraits of his father-in-law in the short time he knew him. The old man talked a lot at these sittings – could be entertaining, even when describing how locks worked. And knobs. He had much to say about knobs. You wouldn't fall asleep listening to him. He was very droll. He'd ask questions to keep you on your toes. 'And are there not vistas through keyholes?' he'd say and all but wink. When he died two years ago Egon was moved enough to made a death mask of him.

*

Sitting there by the fire, he now felt bad about the drawings he had just made. Nothing to do with merit. He knew they were good. He didn't need Edi's permission to draw her, but he had always listened to her comments. Mostly he did as she asked. In salacious poses, fewer and fewer as time went on, she had said that the figure should be given a different face. If it was a whore pose, it should have a whore's face. Not Edi's face. But now that she had no say in the matter he felt it was wrong, devious.

It was difficult to tear himself away from the stove. Clutching his blankets around him, he walked as best he could to the room where Edi lay. Her face looked like it had been made of discoloured wax. He picked the drawings off the dressing table. Stooped to pick the ones that had spilled to the floor – all the time holding the knot of the blanket at his throat so as it would not slip off his shoulders. His knees shook at each step, he shouldered the walls without noticing. He thought of a friend of his, a collector of his work, who had said to him – please do not put anything you draw on the fire. No matter how trivial a sketch it seems. I want you to write in chalk on your stove, so it will never escape your notice, no matter how drunk you are, 'The stove equals me.' And he patted and pointed to his chest. 'You got that? Me.'

He went back to the kitchen, pulled the bentwood armchair closer to the fire, unlatched the stove door. The roar from the firebox was loud but he knew it would not last for long. He stuffed one drawing after another into the flames. After each one he said 'sorry' or 'forgive me'. He wasn't sure whether he said it or thought it. '*Mea culpa*' came to him. He had these fragments of Catholicism still floating in his bloodstream. Probably from his mother's convent education. Little ejaculations she would come out with – 'Lord above', 'Holy St Anthony', 'Mercy me'. He loved using this religious thread in his work. Exaggerating it. Making much of little. He liked it best when there was an element of icon in the work – a kind of visual sarcasm – mocking the religious subjects he portrayed. The St Sebastian drawing with his own likeness pinioned with harpoons; most recently the parody of the Last Supper for the Secession poster, with him at the head of the table where Christ would be. In earlier years, painting heads with Klimt-like gold haloes. His self-portraits with their iconography of hands – each with five fingers splayed like a splash. What they were capable of – caress or punch. Where they'd been. What they could wring from another.

He picked up the remaining drawings of Edi and stuffed them into the flames. And each one constituted a conflagration, a flaring as it reduced each page to blackness. He imagined the fragments, light as black feathers, lifting into the chimney, into the night air, before settling over the whole of the city of Vienna. Black snow falling on the Danube. Soot becoming clogged in the golden foliage of the Secession Building. Darkening the Opera house. The cafés and hotels. The back streets and brothels.

The flames consuming his drawings reminded him of a time he'd been in court. An artist on trial? Who would believe such a thing? It still rankled. For him it was a time of great energy, 'I must investigate new things when I see them,' he was saying to friends. 'I want to taste dark water and see threshing trees and howling winds.' The case was being heard by a toad of a judge (he'd nicknamed him Pontius Pilate) – and 'Your Honourable Toad' ended up burning one of his drawings. He'd been arrested on a 'public immorality' charge, for having his erotic drawings where children could see them. They were nothing out of the ordinary – the odd naked girl, couples – of both men and women – what makes the world go round. The one the judge chose to burn said more about the judge than it did about what he thought was pornographic – an underage girl displaying herself – showing the red flag, you might say. Much head-turning, much whispering, 'What's the old man up to this time?' Such a fuss as the clerk brought in a lit candle and a bucket. Clear to see the judge's desire to hold up the drawing, to show it to the court – but also clear to see was his realisation that he would make himself a promoter of such material. In the end he applied the candle flame to the corner of the page. The paper catching fire. Then when it was just about to get out of hand – he dismissed the clerk, told him to carry away his smoking bucket. The judge fanning the smell of burnt paper away from his face, as if it was the drawing itself that stank. 'Degenerate,' he kept repeating, 'utterly degenerate', while going through a mime of washing his hands. Is that really the most he could say about such work? The accused had wanted to shout, 'To censor an artist is a crime' but he was afraid the judge would just increase his sentence in retaliation. Toad-face locked him up for a total of twenty-four days – although he'd been inside already for twenty-one of them. It was the most miserable time of his life.

His head was pounding. He pressed his eyes with his fingers. Then, when the last drawing was burned, he fell asleep. He did not know for how long. Dreams came to him and mixed with memories and other stuff. His bare-armed mother, her sleeves rolled, washing him in a tin bath. And as she dried him, he became very hungry and she allowed him to eat the flaking wood where the glass and casement met. The child picked with his fingers and packed his mouth with the dry fragments. He was in jail, and his lover at the time – Wally – was kind to him and brought him his art materials and, once, a fresh orange. For days he did not eat it. Instead he stared at it. Like it was a lamp in the gloom of his cell. Then one day he did a watercolour of it, in the grey and blue blankets on his bunk. He salivated as he painted it. And it made him remember the light he had found on his skirting board some mornings ago, which had led him to the keyhole, which in turn had led him to the blinding roomful of sunlight. Wally was so good. He had loved her dearly.

And there was the sound of a door opening and closing and a shaking of his shoulder and a voice.

'God save all here,' said the voice. He awoke and looked up. It was Anton Peschka, his brother-in-law. 'How are things, Egon?' he asked. Egon shook his head, ran his hand through his hair. 'How is Edi?'

Egon stood shakily and took Anton by the elbow, telling him, as best he could, what had happened during the night. He led him to where Edith lay. Anton wept, seeing her like that on the bed.

'She was such a darling,' he said.

Egon stood, his head bowed, seeing the other man's tears. He was exhausted and sat down on the sheer side of the library steps. 'I don't feel well. I think I must have caught it.' Anton put his hand on his brother-in-law's shoulder and squeezed, tried to comfort him. But also tried to avoid getting too close. Egon spoke, but found it difficult, gulping for air in mid-sentence.

'Could you go . . . across the road . . . and tell her mother . . . and sister?'

'Of course.'

Anton straightened Edi's body on the mattress, but Egon could see the caution with which he touched her.

'Where can I get a clean sheet?'

Egon told him where. When Anton left the room, Egon's head sunk until his chin rested on his chest. He leaned against the library pole and was almost asleep by the time his brother-in-law came back with a folded sheet. Anton took away the soiled and bloodied pillow between finger and thumb and dropped it in the corner. He shook out the ironed sheet with its straight creases and allowed it to descend slowly to cover Edith's body. Egon remembered watching Lucille ironing this particular sheet.

'Would you not go to bed?' said Anton.

Egon shook his head. No.

'Can I get you anything? A drink of some sort?'

Egon shook his head again. No.

Anton then took his brother-in-law back to the kitchen and returned him to his chair beside the stove. 'I might be some time. To get an undertaker, and so forth . . . I believe they're busy. And the authorities will have to be informed . . . '

But by this time Egon's head had gone down again. He heard a door closing behind him. And he was in the street, looking this way and that. He began travelling where he had no wish to go. And he had forgotten his luggage. And he had no ticket. And he did not speak the language. No matter how hard he tried, he could not make himself understood. People laughed aloud at his attempts. A woman holding her extravagant blue hat tight to her head stood in front of him, mocking the way he spoke. Her travel coat was covered with flies and insects, which gleamed like sucked jewellery. Turquoise, sapphire, ruby. They bred so quickly they would take over the world, she implied. That would be an improvement, he tried to say but the words would not come out. He dreamed this dream again and again – exactly the same each time, like watching a film at the cinema night after night. They would take over the world. A door slammed and wakened him. A man stood in front of him. His face was covered with a white mask. He put both his hands on Egon's shoulders.

'Easy, boy. Take it easy, Egon.' There seemed to be little or no recognition. 'It's Anton. I was in earlier.' There were noises behind Anton in the passageway. The shuffling of feet, the sound of women's voices. 'I have Edi's mother with me.' The other voice was Edi's sister, Adele. 'I'll take them to her. Sit where you are.' Egon managed to twist his neck around. Frau Harms had improvised a mask with a pale scarf lapped about her lower face. She came across to Egon.

'I'm so sorry,' she said. 'How awful for you. And my poor Edith.'

Egon took a fit of coughing and the old woman moved away from him. He coughed so badly he hurt himself. A crown of thorns around his head. A spear in his side. Anton led the way to the bedroom where Edith lay.

Egon's teeth began to chatter. Maybe he *should* go to bed. Cover himself from head to toe with blankets, because he felt frozen to the marrow of his bones. Take some beef tea, if he could get it. As hot as possible. Anton returned to the kitchen, allowing the two women time to be alone with Edi.

Egon was now in a place where he could not separate what he dreamed from what was real. He pointed to the remaining wood scraps. Anton's voice telling him they had found some coal at the Harms' place. The clank of a bucket handle. Anton opening the stove, piling in the wood fragments and topping up with coal. Allowing the draught to roar in response – the coal to burn. And when it was going full tilt, he opened the door to let the heat into the room. To thaw the fever. And Egon staring. Leaning forward, trying to get a breath. He felt the constriction rising in his chest. He knew now that very soon he was going to die.

But he had done enough. Drawn marvels. Had created more than many another artist had done in a lifetime. Created things never seen in galleries before. He was aware that he was an only son, knew he was the last of the name. Each drawing had his name compressed and embedded in a box placed adroitly for exposure, as if it was about to explode and reveal its maker's name to the world. Anton brought him a glass of water from the sink and although he hadn't demanded it, he was grateful for it. Swallowing it down, his Adam's apple moving at each gulp. When he finished, Egon's head went down again to stare at the fire. Then he saw something that intrigued him. It looked the colour of metal in a blacksmith's forge. Glowing red but not losing its shape. Waving the red flag, you might say. And he recognised the silhouette of a keyhole that had fallen from the wood of the door in flames. And the vista he saw through it was the art he had made and the wonder of it all.

THE DUST GATHERER

Before the woods they came to a fence. On the other side of it was a field of some kind. Grasses – wheat or barley. He hadn't a clue about such things. But he was taken by the structure of the plants. The way they swayed, the rustling sound they made when the wind moved them. They were not yet ripe, still very green for the time of year. He clambered over the fence, plucked one and re-joined her. He threshed the stem about a little, looked down at it as they walked. The head was composed of neatly aligned seeds and long whiskers. He drew the stalk between his fingers, felt its smoothness, its silky feel.

'Do you know what this is?' he asked her.

'Nope.'

He held it up for her to look at closely. Still she shook her head. It had been her suggestion that they go for a walk.

'This is so lovely,' she said. She asked him his name.

'Chris,' he said. He wanted to kiss her but he didn't know if he could kiss her well enough. Maybe she would laugh? Or even smile – that's not how you do it. In his life there was nowhere to practise. No one he could ask.

He drew the stalk through his fingers the opposite way and found that he could not move it at all. The whiskers snagged and wouldn't budge. He explained to her what he had discovered. He looked as closely as he could, but could see no explanation as to why the plant would move smoothly one way through his fingers and be totally blocked when moved in the opposite direction – against the grain. He said this to her. She looked at him with raised eyebrows.

'I like "against the grain",' he said. 'It's a kinda joke.'

'You're interested in such weird things,' she said.

'Why's it weird? To want to know stuff.'

'Even if it's unimportant?'

'I just asked.'

She folded her arms in front of her and paced slowly and deliberately, looking downwards at her sandalled feet. Her toenails were painted red.

'It's *big* things that really get me,' she said.

'Like?'

'Where do we go when we die?'

'We don't go anywhere. We stay put. Become dust – disintegrate.'

'You've a great fondness for big words.'

Still fiddling with the plant, he joined his hands behind his back.

'My father died not so long ago.'

'Oh, I'm sorry. If I'd known I . . . ' Her words disappeared before she finished what she was going to say.

In the distance they could hear shouts from the others. It was getting dark and someone was lighting a fire on the beach. They could not see it but could smell the driftwood burning. And hear the snapping as bigger bits were broken to fit the fire. The guy with the guitar had started up 'Shake, Rattle and Roll'.

As they walked side-by-side the back of their wrists touched once. The boy apologised and she dismissed it as nothing. For a long time afterwards he felt the brush of her skin, was aware that she had a wristwatch on. A strategy to hold her hand occurred to him.

'What time is it?' It seemed natural to lift her hand. The light was fading and he bent closer to see. 'I like your watch.'

'Thank you,' she said. But he had not the courage to go on holding her hand and let it drop by her side.

Chris heard it distinctly in the dark when the summer storm was at its height. He and his younger brother, Leo, slept in the back bedroom. It was a noise very hard to describe: thrumming, otherworldly. Breath across strings – the worst gusts hummed as far as the bedroom.

'What do you think that is?'

Leo was sound asleep, so they couldn't compare notes. He smiled at 'compare notes'.

At first he thought it was maybe a dream. Then he knew what it was – when an old flowerpot was toppled and fell with a crash among the strings.

The next morning Granda sat at the kitchen table, spooning porridge into him. When Chris came in the old man said, 'That was some night. Did you get any sleep at all?'

Chris played along with him and shook his head – no, he didn't. His mother brought fresh tea from the scullery.

'The window frames rattled all night,' Granda said. 'At about five I had to get up and wedge them with a bit of cardboard.'

Bits of leaves had blown off the tree in the chapel drive that overhung their back yard. They were stuck all over the kitchen window and gave anyone sitting at the table a sickly green pallor. Chris made toast with a long fork at the fire. He spread it with jam. As his mother joined them she glanced up at the window.

'Lord God,' she said. 'Would you look at that?'

'What's that, Eileen?'

She pointed. There was a slate jutting over the edge of next door's guttering. They lived in a terrace of cheek-by-jowl red-brick Victorian houses and their yard was hemmed in by their own roof and next door's.

'Dangerous,' said Granda, craning to look up. 'Could take the head clean off you.'

'Watch yourselves getting coal,' she said.

'Or out at the piano,' said Chris.

'Don't think that's an excuse for not getting on with it,' said his mother. 'There's only a week of the summer holidays left and I want that piano out of there.'

'Somebody might appreciate it,' said Granda.

'You couldn't *give* it away,' said Eileen. 'God knows, I've tried.'

When they had finished she began to clear the table. She shouted from the scullery.

'Away and waken that brother of yours. He's a disgrace, lying in his bed till this hour.'

Chris shouted upstairs but got no response. Eventually he had to go up and give his brother a shake. Leo turned in the bed and pulled the clothes up to protect himself.

When Chris came down he went out into the yard. He looked up at the precarious slate. His mother joined him, her arms folded, her face squinting against the light.

'You'll come to no harm,' she said. The boy pulled a face. 'When you were out gallivanting last night somebody called at the door for you.'

'Who?'

His mother gave a slow shrug.

'Did he give his name?'

'It was a girl.'

'What?'

'A girl – you know, girls. You're fifteen years of age.'

'Who was it?'

'How would I know? She was brazen enough not to say.'

The leaves of the tree in the chapel yard made a shushing noise as the wind moved through them. His mother went back into the kitchen. She shouted over her shoulder, 'She said she'd call back sometime.'

The boy blushed and turned to face the piano. The lid was open and he peered down into its guts. Its array of hammers – some missing, the gaps obvious. He couldn't resist putting his finger in and plucking at the strings. He did the same thing every time he went for a shovel of coal. Except in the dark. He was afraid of what might have crawled in there. He liked the plucked sound better than hitting the keys in the normal way. That only reminded him how out of tune the instrument actually was. He repeated the plucking action with different strings. Thicker and thinner. Higher and lower. There were some strings that did not resonate but produced a dead clunk sound.

No girl had ever called at the house before. Ever. Who was she? What could she want? He didn't know any girl well enough. In fact, if he was honest, he hardly knew any girls at all.

The keyboard lid was open and some of the keys had lost their ivories. Wood brown beneath, like missing teeth. The flowerpot he'd heard falling in the night was upended above the piano strings, granules of soil spilled everywhere. He got a hatchet and a rusty hammer out of the coalhouse. Evenly weighted, he faced the target. Then he noticed that the brass candle-holders had disappeared. It could only have been Leo. There were chisel marks on the upright panelling where they had been parted from the wood.

He swung the hatchet but it skated off the dark varnished wood. He inserted the blade into the joint between front and side and began hammering it deeper and deeper, using the blade as a wedge. Each time he struck he heard the strings vibrate. And the deeper it went, the louder the cracking sound became as the fracture widened.

When he was very young and the piano was in tune, his mother had offered him a choice of learning to play or going to elocution. Chris loathed both options. So, on the toss of a coin, he went to elocution. But after a couple of months – being made to say things slowly and in a posh voice – he swore he'd never go back. He spent his bus fare on a Highland toffee bar and sat in Alexandra

Park, his jaw rotating, until it was time to go home again. Three weeks passed before the elocution teacher – a woman who could make anyone feel they were from the back of beyond – phoned to ask if the boy was ill.

His mother, panting with distress, confronted him when he came in.

'Where were you?'

'Elocution.'

'Indeed you were not. For she's just off the phone, asking where you were this last couple of weeks. Do you think I have money to burn?'

Her anger, and silence, continued for weeks.

He pulled the facing board towards him and, with one wrench, tore away the front panel. The unvarnished wood inside was stained into peaks and troughs by the night's rain. He set the panel against the wall at forty-five degrees and began jumping on it. But it just acted as a springboard, catapulting him off. He tried stamping to break it but that didn't work, either. He turned to the piano again. Small swings of the hatchet cut pale slivers away from the edges. When he had enough together, he brought a bundle in to burn on the fire. But Leo was making his toast and didn't want a lot of flames.

'It's a bit of a waste anyway,' said his mother. 'They'd do for kindling in the morning.'

'Listen to who's talking about waste,' said Granda. 'It's an out-and-out shame – the whole bloody thing.'

'It darkened every room it ever sat in,' said Eileen. 'Nothing but an oul dust gatherer.'

'Not in my day, it wasn't,' said Granda.

'Aye, there was no dust in those days.'

'And I have the receipt to prove it. From Crane's Showroom. Ninety-one pounds. It's up the stairs.'

'What would that be worth today?' asked Leo.

'After Sunday-evening devotions,' said Granda, 'a whole crowd would come back to our place for a sing-song. Most of them from the choir. So many good voices round the piano. And your daddy vamping away. We lived in Antrim at the time. "The Constitutional Movement must go on" was the favourite, would you believe?'

'For God's sake.' Eileen rolled her eyes to the ceiling. 'How far back can you go?'

'To the beginning.' He looked around him, then spoke as if talking only to the two boys. 'And the young ones would be on the lookout for the last bus to Belfast. Then there'd be a mad scramble for coats and hats, when it appeared at the top of the hill.'

'That was then. This is today,' said Eileen.

'What about the piano stool?'

'It's firewood this ages,' she said. He sighed. 'You never even noticed it was gone.'

'And all the sheet music?'

'And all the sheet music,' said Eileen. 'What good's sheet music on its own?'

Granda was Chris' father's father. He was well liked by everyone who came into the house. The only one to fight with him was Eileen.

'You've a great head of hair for your age, but no sense,' she told him.

'What's the const . . . constit?' Leo asked.

'Home Rule,' said Granda. 'Ireland looking after itself. Running things without British by-your-leave.'

Chris went back out into the yard. Leo came after him eating a piece of toast. He set his sugary tea on a windowsill.

'Fuck sake,' he said quietly.

'What?'

'That slate.'

'Ma says it'd take another storm to bring it down.'

Chris pointed to what he'd just done.

'The front panel and the one below came away, dead easy,' he said.

Leo pushed in the rest of his toast and chewed, his mouth open.

'Did you take those candlesticks off?'

'Naw. Not me,' said Leo. He stepped forward and withdrew a long ivory key from the piano.

'How'd you know how to do that?'

'Look at the length,' Leo said. He turned it over in his hand, looked along it. Balanced it on his finger, watched it see-saw. '*En garde*,' he said and took up a fencing stance. He nodded to Chris to arm himself.

Chris lifted another long key from the bed of keys. They crossed swords. Fenced a bit to and fro, until their mother knocked on the window and shouted at them to stop the carrying-on.

Something fell from Leo's sword. It rolled around the sloping yard. He picked it up and weighed it in his hand.

'What is it?' said Chris.

'Bloody metal.' Leo turned it over. 'Lead? It's very heavy.' He turned over the key in his hand and saw the circular hole where the lead had come from. 'I know a scrappy in Mountcollyer.'

'The Prods'll give you a doing, if they catch you going down there.'

Leo slotted the disc into the hole, then replaced the key. He pressured it and the note sounded – distinctly off-key – but it played. Leo watched the movement when he played it repeatedly. 'The weight is to stop it sticking. So the key can go back where it came from.'

'We did fulcrums in physics,' said Chris. 'Maybe it's fulcra?'

'You mean see-saws,' said Leo. 'The hammers look like slices of bananas.' He struck the key and watched while one slice darted forward and hit the string. The sound came and the key returned to its place. He repeatedly did this. Ding-ding-ding-ding-ding . . .

'Pretty neat, eh?'

Chris nodded.

Eileen shouted from the scullery, 'What did I say? Will you please get on with it.'

Leo stopped pounding the note. There was silence.

'Were you here last night when the girl called at the door?' said Chris.

'Naw. There was a girl at our door?'

'So you have no idea who it was?'

'Not a clue.'

That night he lay awake thinking about her. It must be her who had called at the door. He didn't know any other girl sufficiently well. That night he'd been serving drinks from the boot of one of the cars. People were talking and there was a lot of laughing going on. Somebody was tuning a guitar somewhere.

'Could I have an orange juice, please,' a voice said.

He looked up and saw her and nodded. She was a real peach, her hair up in a ponytail. He made the drink and diluted it and passed it to her. She smiled her thanks. He didn't know her name but thought her face was familiar. She circled around, speaking to anybody and everybody, sipping her drink. He said to the guy next in line, 'Who's she?'

'D'you not know Paula? You must be about the only one.'

He wondered what age she was – would he make a fool of himself if he spoke to her? What if she turned to him and said something like: I don't normally speak to boys who are still at school. After a while she came back for another drink.

'That was quick.'

'I'm thirsty.'

'Paula's a terrible drouth,' said a voice. She shoved the boy who said it.

'How dare you,' she said. 'And me a Pioneer.'

Chris poured her a second orange juice and they began to talk, leaning against the side of the car.

After a while she said, 'Are you done here?' He shrugged, not sure. 'Fancy a walk? Or would that be deserting your post?'

A guy came up and poured himself a vodka and orange and nodded his thanks. It got that people began to pour their own drinks.

On the walk she had come out with a torrent of talk, so much so that he thought she was nervous, when in reality it was him who was shaking inside.

Turning in bed, he shuddered. Why had he told her about the death of his father? What kind of tact was that? Sheer stupidity, when all he wanted to do was kiss her. Her face said, I am open and friendly and you would do well to get to know me and one day . . . who knows?

Everybody said his father had been such a good, deeply religious man. One of his father's friends, an old artist, had almost made him cry one day in the street when he said, 'Your father was a darling man.' Chris had muttered thanks and shouldered past. He had swallowed and swallowed. There was a hardness in his throat he couldn't get rid of. But that wouldn't happen to him now. Nowadays he had more control. Could think about him without going to pieces.

His father had loved many things – but there seemed to be two things in particular: Ireland and singing. He had loads of records of famous singers stored in the sitting room, sheathed in albums that looked like books. Each page had a round hole at its centre to display the label. John McCormack singing 'When Other Lips', Richard Tauber, 'You Are My Heart's Delight', Heddle Nash singing 'Silent Worship'. Some of the records were accompanied by orchestras, others by the piano. For ages Chris thought that the man singing was also playing the piano.

And Ireland? What about Ireland? 'If there was one thing that really got his goat,' said Eileen, 'it was the unionist government threatening the jail for anyone flying the Irish flag. "*In Ireland,*" he always said.' When they were clearing out his stuff after he died they found a postcard he'd made. On it he'd painted a tricolour of red, black and purple. In the centre of the black panel was a white dot and the viewer was invited, in their father's stately handwritten instructions, to stare at this for sixty seconds – then switch their gaze to a black dot below. And there, hovering and insubstantial, would be the green, white and gold of Ireland. Written at the bottom of the page was 'They cannot put you in jail for a flag of the mind.'

His mother always went to nine o'clock Mass on Sunday, telling everyone there was work to be done, dinners to be made and – in this case – pianos to be dismantled. Chris said he was going to half-ten. But of late he passed the end of the chapel drive and continued on to his bolt-hole in Alexandra Park. He would sit with his hands in his pockets and his feet straight out in front of him. There was no God. There was bad luck and there was good luck. The bench gave him a panoramic view – he could see who was coming, who was going. Was it someone who would later talk to his mother? Not with any malice but just drop him in it somehow – 'I saw Chris in the park on Sunday morning' kind of thing. This was his hideout when he'd skipped elocution. It would be catastrophic if his mother found out he was also skipping Mass. Sometimes she would ask a series of casual questions when he came back to the house.

'Who said Mass? Did he preach? What was the sermon about?' This was not a grilling, it was what passed for conversation. He had to have answers.

To vary the routine that summer, some Sundays he would walk round the ponds in the Waterworks, watch people sailing their model yachts. If it was raining he would shelter in nearby Queen Mary Gardens – there was a dry place where the old ones played draughts or read the Sunday papers, but none of them knew his mother. There was a clock there he could keep his eye on. In the park he could hear church bells at eleven o'clock. Whether they were Catholic bells or not, he didn't know. But it gave him just enough time to walk back to see the congregation coming out the main doors of the chapel like a crowd spilling from a football ground. He mingled with his school mates.

'Who said Mass?'

'Father Ferry.'

'Are ye mitching Mass again, ya bastard?'

Chris laughed.

'Was there a sermon?'

'He seemed in a bit of a rush.'

If there had been a sermon he would have had to get the gist of it. On this particular Sunday he saw the girl he'd walked with at the barbecue. Paula. She was coming down the steps carrying a missal, wearing a beret tugged to one side and talking to an old woman. Paula changed the missal to her other hand and gave the old woman her arm to lean on. The two of them went to the wooden lean-to that sold the Irish Sunday papers. English papers you had to buy elsewhere because of the filth in them. Paula bought a paper for the old woman and handed it to her, along with her change. Then she straightened up and looked around her. Chris turned his back, lowered his head and concentrated on talking to his friends. But he was distracted by a blush coming on, felt it creeping up his neck and into his face.

'What's the beamer for?'

'Nuthin',' Chris shook his head. 'Have you your English homework done?'

'Have you?'

'No. Haven't even thought about it yet.'

His mother didn't ask him any detective-like questions during Sunday dinner. After eating, the brothers went into the yard, past Granda, who had fallen asleep in his armchair. They stood facing the remains of the piano. Leo set to work withdrawing the long keys and snapping them over his knee, then making a small wigwam of them on the floor of the yard.

'Getting smaller,' said Chris. 'Like a carcass in the wild.'

'Plundered,' said Leo.

Chris tried to play 'Chopsticks' from a standing position. But got very little sound out of it. The keys felt limp.

'It wasn't like this yesterday,' he said.

'It's dying.'

Chris withdrew one of the keys from the key bed. It felt light. He turned it over and saw that the lead counterweight was missing. The same with the next one.

'Did you take all the weights out?'

'Me. Naw.'

'Somebody did.' Chris stared at his brother. 'Somebody who knows a scrappy where he can flog them.'

'Get on with it.' Leo had eaten too much and now took great delight in belching.

'And the pedals,' said Chris. 'Somebody's taken the brass pedals.' He bent and looked closely up into the piano. 'And their fucking brass rods.' He hissed, so his mother wouldn't hear.

Then he remembered seeing Leo a couple of days ago with two full-colour American war comics.

'Where did you get them?'

Leo had shrugged – said one of his mates had lent them to him.

'You're fuckin' at it.'

From beneath the piano he thought he heard the front-door bell. He hushed Leo with his hand. A moment later the back door opened and his mother put her head out.

'Somebody for you, Christopher.' She raised both her eyebrows at once and gave a weird sort of a grin.

Chris moved through the scullery and kitchen into the hallway. The vestibule door was almost shut but he could see a brightly coloured figure through the patterned glass. He looked at himself in the mirror in the hallstand and tried to smooth his hair. He opened the door.

'Paula,' he said. 'Hi.'

'Good to see you,' she said. 'I saw you outside Mass this morning – but you were away before I had a chance to talk to you.' He looked over his shoulder, then stepped out into the vestibule, pulling the door almost closed.

'So how have you been?'

'Good.'

Both of them were smiling.

'Maybe this is a bad time . . . ' she said.

'Naw. I'm just working. On the piano.'

'I'm sorry I didn't know.'

'What?'

'That you could play.'

'Naw – naw. I can't play. "Chopsticks" mebbe, but I can . . .'

There was a shout of his mother's voice from deep inside the house.

'Bring your guest in. You can't keep her on the doorstep.'

Chris backed into the door and it swung open and he invited Paula in.

His mother was coming up the hallway.

'Where's your manners?' she said to him. She shook Paula's hand, held her hand in both of hers. 'I'm Eileen, Christopher's mum.'

'How do you do? Delighted to meet you. I'm Paula.'

Eileen pushed open the sitting-room door and invited the girl in, making a sweeping gesture. Chris stood blushing in the hall. Sometimes his mother could be a total cringe.

He wondered what on earth this girl saw in him. The night of the barbecue – and now calling a second time for him at the house. His mother waved goodbye with her fingers and backed off. Chris moved into the sitting room and closed the door to make sure his mother was excluded. He stood facing Paula, his hands behind his back. Again he wanted to kiss her but he didn't know the moves. All he knew was hesitancy. How did you start? How did you avoid the slap in the face that sometimes happened in movies? She was so attractive. Her style, her face, her make-up. She wore a crisp white blouse. Her breasts nudged forward against the white and betrayed the pattern of the material beneath. A print skirt with a black wasp belt, which was held together with hooks and eyes. She had a different watch to the one she was wearing the night of the barbecue. But maybe it was just a different-coloured strap.

'So?' said Chris. By this time his knees were trembling. He hoped she wouldn't notice. He'd have a better chance if they were sitting down. 'Have a seat.'

'Thank you.' She smoothed her skirt as she sank into an armchair.

'That's not the same watch.'

'You noticed.' Her voice was high-pitched with surprise. 'In our house it's what they buy you for birthdays. If they can't think of anything else.'

'I'm getting one for my next birthday.' There was a long silence. 'What can I do for you?' he said.

'There was something . . . ' Paula said. She hesitated. 'It was just a favour. It struck me when I saw you at Mass this morning. I'm in the Legion of Mary and our branch of the Praesidium in the parish here is running a recruitment drive. How would you like to come along? Meet Father Ferry. Come as a probationer. See if you'd *like* to join.'

'I've heard of it, but . . . what does it . . . ?'

'Corporal and spiritual works of mercy. We pray and we do as much good as we can for others.'

He sat staring at her. She wasn't after him at all. It was his soul she was after, if he had one. He wanted to cover his head in his hands and be sitting on his park bench. He didn't know what to say to her.

'Eh . . . '

'Have you ever flown?' she said.

'No,' he shook his head.

'D'you fancy it?'

Chris nodded, not sure.

'Well, this is your chance. The parish helps fly sick people to Lourdes. It would count as one of your corporal works of mercy. You'd help look after them in the plane, and wheel them about the grotto. And the basilica. Keep their spirits up. D'you do French?'

'*Oui.*' They both laughed.

'Well then,' she said, as if that was that.

'But if they were from here, they'd speak English,' said Chris.

'Very badly,' she said and they both laughed again.

'I don't believe in stuff like Lourdes.'

'Why not? The evidence is all there. Ask Father Ferry.'

'And I'm no good at joining things. Remember I told you about me doing elocution. Or *not* doing it. That was a disaster.'

'A cup and saw-sir.' She *had* remembered.

'Also, I'm not so sure I believe in God all that much. To get involved.'

'That's . . . ' she hesitated, 'sad. Have you talked this through with anybody? Father Ferry is really very good. Might be a reason for you to come along to the Praesidium meeting. There's a discussion section. Which might help.'

'It's kind of fundamental,' he said. 'Discussions don't help with things as blindingly obvious as that.' He couldn't meet her eye. She remained silent. He heard the slither of the material of her dress as she rearranged herself to face him.

'Let's just say I have planted a seed. Father Ferry is a known theologian – I'm sure he can help.' She looked at her watch. It was on the wrong side of her thin wrist and she turned it to face her. 'At the door you said you were working on the piano. If you can't play, what exactly are you doing?'

Chris pointed to the alcove, then down to the floor-boards.

'See these marks. That's where it was.'

'I don't know what you're talking about.'

'The piano. The dents in the floor – where the castors were. Me and my brother Leo are just getting rid of it. In the yard. D'you want to see?'

She pulled a strange, laughing face.

'Whatever you say.'

Chris knew immediately it was a mistake. He led her in through the kitchen – past Granda, who was still asleep in his chair. She made a face that meant, 'I'm as silent as can be so's he will not wake.' Her skirt was flared and she had to turn sideways to thread her way through the furniture as she followed Chris. There was a smell of cooked cabbage, the sink still full of dirty dishes.

'Don't look at the mess,' said Eileen.

'You should see our house,' said Paula.

Chris opened the scullery door and led her out into the yard.

'This way,' he said.

Leo looked up, surprised to see such a creature in his own surroundings. Paula said hello but didn't shake hands. Maybe he looked too young. Her heels made a sound Chris had never heard before, clicking on the tiles of the yard. She walked around the stricken piano, touched it. Did what everybody did, plucking a string with her nail.

'Look at the size of it,' she said. 'How did you get it out here?'

Eileen stepped from the scullery.

'A certain amount of charm was required,' she said. 'I knew these two hadn't got it in them, so I went round to the chapel one night – devotions – and offered tea and buns to any man who'd give us a lift with it. I got six takers. Plus my two boys. Turned out to be a good night. Good crack over the tea and buns. They didn't all know each other, but by the end of the night they were the best of pals. There was a lot more space in the sitting room afterwards.'

However careful, Paula must have disturbed Granda and he appeared out into the yard to see what all the fuss was about. Eileen introduced Paula to him. Unable to move much in the crowded yard, Granda bowed his head in the girl's direction. Then he looked up.

'Mind that loose slate,' he said.

Paula looked up and saw the dark overhang. She smiled and covered the top of her head with her hand.

Granda started to laugh. He tried to kid her on, 'I think it's shifted,' he said. 'If it fell now, none of us would be spared.'

'What are we all doing out here anyway?' said Eileen.

'Viewing the desecration,' said Granda.

'We're only tempting fate,' said Eileen, making shooing motions with her hands. 'Everybody back in.'

They all shuffled back into the house. Paula stood in the scullery, looking around her. Eileen took up the dishcloth and shoved her sleeves a little higher up on her arms.

'Can I help?' said Paula.

'With what?'

'The dishes.'

'Not at all. You're all right, love.'

'I'll dry.'

The mother paused. She pursed her mouth, then accepted the girl's offer.

'No, you wash and I'll dry. I know where things go. It's very good of you. It's more than any of my sons would do. Do you hear that, boys,' she roared after them. 'But only if you put on an apron. I'd hate to see anything happen to your Sunday best.'

Paula put her head into the halter of a clean white apron and her hands whirled as she tied it behind her. Chris could hear the talk between Paula and his mother still going on and on. Sometimes he could make out what they were saying, but other times it was drowned in the rattle of plates and cutlery. What was not in doubt was the laughter between them. Their polite voices.

Leo got up and went into the front room and came out with a window pole. The hook on the end of it was brass.

'What are you going to do with that?' said Chris.

Leo went past them into the scullery and came out carrying the indoor sweeping brush as well. He liked to boast they were a two-brush family. There was a yard brush with stiff bristles, which lived in the coalhole, and an indoor brush, which was much softer.

'What's going on?'

Leo ran up the stairs. The two women in the kitchen continued to talk and work and occasionally laugh. They both agreed that Father Ferry was the nicest of men. Both cited instances of proof for his goodness. And there was no better confessor. No nebbing into your affairs. He'd just give you your penance and that was that. Next, please. The two women argued affectionately over which of them was the worst sinner. Granda sat in the armchair, where he got the drift of the conversation coming from the scullery. He raised his eyebrows. Chris now felt responsibility for Paula, for showing her out of the house politely. While he was waiting he eased himself onto a wooden chair.

There was a shout from upstairs. Leo's voice ringing down from the top landing.

'Nobody go out into the yard.'

'Did you hear that?' Chris shouted to the women in the scullery.

'What?'

'Leo says nobody's to go out into the yard.'

'In the name of God – why?'

Everyone started to look up, to see what Leo was doing. They heard the top bedroom window open. Then Paula saw the window pole coming out. It seemed to extend for ever.

'He's tied it to the brush,' Eileen said. From her position she couldn't see properly. 'Jesus, Mary and Joseph. He's not out on the roof, is he?'

'No.'

The brass hook clumsily made its way towards the loose slate.

'Chris, go up and give him a hand,' Eileen shouted. 'You've a bigger reach than him.'

Chris raced up the stairs two at a time. In the back bedroom, Leo stood on a chair, trying to manoeuvre the tied-together poles out the top of the window. Chris stood listening to his own panting.

'It'll never work.'

'It will.'

Chris noticed his brother's mouth, the tongue pointed and peeping out the side.

'If it does, are you gonna charge them a fee?'

Leo said nothing, concentrating. The soft hairs of the sweeping brush were close to his face and getting in his way. Now Chris could see that the straightness of the device was under strain and it was beginning to sag at the join.

'Hold the brush,' said Leo. Chris did as he was told. Leo got his head and one shoulder completely out of the window and had more control. He managed to insert the brass hook beneath the exposed edge of the slate, then made an upward movement. Nothing happened. Only the tied joint of the poles flexed and moved. Then it happened. A scraping sound – and the slate began to move. It cleared the guttering and for a second there was silence, before an almighty crash. There was a noise like the hum of a struck tuning fork from the piano, which went on for some time.

'Sheer genius,' said Leo. But then in his attempt to withdraw the window pole, its hook caught on the edge of another slate and dislodged it. 'Fuck it.' Leo paused and looked at the damage. This slate had been loosened, but it did not overhang the guttering. 'Don't tell them. They'll not see it from down there.'

'But it's dangerous,' said Chris.

'It's up to next door.'

'But it's us who'll get killed.'

Leo stepped off the chair and Chris took his place. He had the strength to open the window a little more and put his head out. He could see the newly dislodged slate. When he looked down into the yard, it was covered in shattered blue-black fragments. Leo withdrew the poles back into the room and loosened the cord binding them. He handed the brush to Chris and said, 'You can sweep it up.'

'Not with this.'

Chris came into the kitchen and put the brush back in the glory hole where it belonged.

'Hi,' he said.

'Hi.'

Paula was washing the cutlery. The water was brown and the suds had disappeared.

Eileen was drying, dropping the items into their correct compartments in the drawer. 'That's why I keep the fire on all day,' she said. 'It gives you all the hot water you want. Use some fresh.'

'In our house we wash the cutlery first. If you do the plates first, then you need to change your water.'

'Ooo,' said Eileen, 'so I'm doing the dishes wrong, am I? After all these years?' Chris sidestepped his way out from between them. The two women seemed to be able to laugh at everything. To kid each other with ease.

He went out into the yard. His first reaction was to look up and see if the slate Leo had just dislodged was visible. It wasn't, but he could feel its presence. He took the yard brush out of the coalhole and began to sweep. The stiff bristles propelled the bits of slate into a heap in the middle of the yard. He swept the lot onto the coal shovel and threw the pieces into the bin. Granda came to watch what he was doing.

'It's a sad sight,' he said, nodding at the piano. He went over to it and drew the back of his nails lightly along the strings. Then he noticed a couple of shards of slate lodged there. He picked them out carefully and heard the reverberation as they were removed. Chris lifted the lid of the bin. It too had its own reverberation, a note. Granda dropped the pieces in. Then they stood in the yard listening. It backed onto the chapel driveway and some children were playing and shouting. The sound of their feet slapping on the tarmac, squeals as they chased after one another.

'Looks and smells like rain,' said Granda. He turned to go into the house. Chris set the brush and shovel back in the coalhole and followed him in.

'Job done,' said Chris. He stepped into the scullery. Paula was just getting out of the apron. Her hair became dishevelled as she peeled the neck of the apron off over her head. She shook it back into place, then patted it more to her liking. His mother offered Paula tea, and Paula refused, said it would only be making more dishes to wash. She said that she'd better get on. She had things to do.

'Don't talk to me,' said his mother. 'I've to go round to the chapel and do the flowers again. They looked a bit wilted this morning at Mass. Better change them for this evening's devotions.'

'Where'll you get fresh flowers today?'

'It's summer – there's plenty getting left in the sacristy. People be that proud when their flowers are used.' Then she broke off and gave the girl a hug. 'You're a darling,' said Eileen.

'Och, it was nothing,' said Paula. 'Ten minutes of my time.' Chris looked at her and the sudden reappearance of her chest. She tightened the black belt at her waist and began to move towards the hall.

'Good for you, Son,' said his mother. She patted him on the back. 'That's a weight off my mind. That slate.'

'It was Leo.'

'You too.'

'I must go,' said Paula. 'It was lovely to meet you all.'

Chris touched her elbow as he guided her into the hall. Eileen shouted a farewell and added, 'Call any time.'

On the front doorstep Paula said, 'Think it over. Joining the Legion. You'd enjoy it.'

'Mebbe,' said Chris.

'See ya,' she said.

'See ya around.'

In the kitchen he sat down on the other side of the fire from Granda. The boy was on the edge of his seat. They could still hear the children playing in the chapel grounds but it was much distanced, now that the yard door was closed. Granda looked across at him.

'Are you all right?'

'Yes.'

'You don't look it.'

'It's maybe the light coming off that tree,' said Chris. 'Makes me look green.'

Granda lit his pipe with a spill from the cut wood on the hearth. His lips popped as he drew in the air and smoke.

'She's a fine lassie,' he said. Chris nodded. 'Far too good for the likes of you. What was her name again?'

'Paula.'

'Paula what?'

'Paula Magee.'

'Would she be anything to the Magees from Clanchattan Street?'

'How would I know?'

'I liked the way she got tore into the work immediately.'

'Aye, she's criminally kind,' said Chris.

Granda laughed.

'Speaking of which,' he said, 'where's Leo?'

'How would I know? I haven't a clue where he is half the time.'

'He has no sense. That slate coulda gone through a window or anything. And that's not the end of it. Somebody'll have to tell next door.'

'What?'

'They'll have a leak in their roof.' Granda's pipe had gone out and he knocked the bowl of it against the bars of the grate. He blew through the pipe to clear it. 'It's time you were starting to shave. Mebbe tidy yourself up a bit.'

Chris rolled his eyes.

'Now he tells me.'

'It's no laughing matter,' said Granda. He carved a little tobacco off the black block with his penknife, then rubbed it between his hands and filled his pipe. There was silence between them. 'That instrument out there. To be in such a state. Your daddy could play a bit. By ear. Never had a lesson in his life. He could vamp, y'know, or accompany people singing.'

For Chris, there were still certain words. The word 'daddy' was one of them. There was silence as Chris tried to rid himself of the feeling in his throat. The thought of somebody singing and his father playing along on the piano, looking up at the singer. Heddle Nash doing 'Silent Worship' maybe. Quietly swallowing and swallowing so that his grandfather wouldn't notice.

'It's funny that,' said Granda.

'What?'

'It still gets me sometimes when I call him your "daddy". It's difficult to say. Because he was my son. And what's more, it takes years before a body can talk about it. It should never happen – a man burying his son.'

The next week the boys went back to school and Eileen phoned the corporation. She politely asked for the metal frame of the piano to be lifted, taken away and dumped. When the boys came in from school on the Friday, it was gone and the yard seemed a larger, emptier place.

WANDERING

She closed the bathroom door but left it unbolted. In the cabinet was an old Christmas present, still unopened. She'd celebrate Friday's news with it. *Wild Meadowlands Relaxing Bath Foam*. Been smiling into herself at every available opportunity since. Maybe the foam was from one of her classes. She splashed some onto the enamel floor of the bath. It smelled good, like a summer night. She began running the water. Both taps. At first it was a thin sound, but gradually it became a roar as the foam built into clouds. Cumulus. The place filled with steam, making the mirror grey. She undressed and hung her things on the back of the door, then inserted her foot through the foam into the water. She snatched it back. Far too hot. Her foot stung and it began to feel red, yet to the eye it was still white. She turned off the hot and increased the cold, rowing the water round the bath with her hand, the foam almost up to her face as she bent over. When she straightened up she thought she heard a noise. She turned off the cold and listened. Nothing but silence. It had sounded like the floorboard on the landing.

She climbed into the bath and lowered herself into the water. Everything rose up the sides, including the foam. Archimedes. And Hitchcock. That bloody Hitchcock was responsible for a lot. In the bathroom, women's vulnerability was complete. Without clothes, without hearing when the shower was on or the taps running, without sight when water got into your eyes. And yet she didn't want to lock the door as some kind of protection. What if she herself were to collapse? And that was not beyond the bounds of possibility. Nobody could get in to help her.

This was a rare indulgence, filling the bath to this depth. She bundled a fluffy towel and put it behind her head and neck as a pillow and lay back. Her knees just showed. It was completely silent now, after the noise of the taps. Only the faint static of the foam as it settled and dwindled. And the occasional clucking and swirling beneath her body when she moved. This was thinking time. Good, valuable thinking time.

She remembered her mother refusing to buy bath foam. Skimping. 'Both you and I know, Vera, it's nothing but a total extravagance. A bath is to get you clean.' Once when she was younger she'd taken an eggcup of washing-up liquid and an egg whisk into the bath with her and, in no time at all, she had mountains of foam. Afterwards her skin felt tight. And when she confessed what she'd done, her mother said it was no bloody wonder. 'If you don't wear rubber gloves when you use that stuff,' she said, 'your skin'll feel like crocodiles.' Seeing her daughter's alarmed face, she patted her on the head and sang the soothing tones of the television advert, 'For hands that do dishes', as if to make everything all right again. Then her mother pulled off the rubber gloves she was wearing and righted them by blowing till the fingers popped out, one by one.

Her mother had sewn her a doll one Christmas – skimping again – saying, as a plus point, it was something that could *not* be bought in the shops. What Vera hated *most* about it was the fact that it *couldn't* be bought in a shop. It meant it was old-fashioned. That meant they were poor. She wanted things that were gleaming and new. Shop things. But gradually she became fond of the doll. A Cinderella – soft, with a sad cloth face. The doll's dress reached the floor and had been made to look tattered. But instead of the doll's feet, there was another doll's head and you could quickly pull the whole thing inside-out. Abracadabra! The inside-out of Cinderella's face was happy and beautiful, as befits a girl at a dance. And the reverse dress was white and sparkled with sequins. A total transformation. A scullery wench ready for the ball. If only it was as easy as that – pulling herself through to the smiling one.

When she came out of the bathroom in her dressing gown the first thing she noticed was two daddy-long-legs circling the landing light. She thought it odd. Going downstairs, she was aware of a draught. The front door was wide to the wall and the place filled with summer insects. Jesus! Ten, twenty daddy-long-legs, tipping the ceiling, colliding crazily with everything. They made a tiny noise, wing-tippings, flutterings, dry paper noises. Their legs were long, making them seem clumsy – like creatures burdened with ironing boards or deckchairs.

'Aw no,' she said, 'where in the name of the shining God is she now?' She turned and went upstairs again. She opened her mother's room and put her head round the door. The bed was empty and the corner of the coverlet thrown back.

She could have kicked herself. She had intended to 'apply the cosh' before her bath but something had distracted her. And then she saw that the old woman was yawning and looking under the pillow for her rosary beads – she seemed just dying to get to sleep. There would be no need for the cosh tonight.

She checked her own room but it was dark and the bed untouched.

'The bird has flown, God damn her.'

She went downstairs and looked out the front door into the evening. One of the daddy-long-legs landed on the wall beside her. She lifted an envelope from the hall table and swatted it, leaving the thing a zigzagged mess. The rest of them she tried to wave out the door with her hands. She hunched her shoulders and tried to retract her head into herself – to make herself less of a target for them. She shuddered and wiped the envelope on the hip of her dressing gown. How long had she lain in the bath? Twenty minutes, half an hour? Long enough to have sensed the water cooling. She had been aware of this several times, and each time turned on the hot tap to beef up the temperature again. But reheating more than twice was an extravagance. And she'd gone through her finishing routine. Twenty minutes rather than half an hour, she guessed.

One last check. There was no point in her rushing out, if she hadn't taken the precaution of searching the house thoroughly. Her mother could be anywhere. So she started at the top of the house and worked her way down.

'Lily?'

Looking beneath beds, opening walk-in cupboards and wardrobes – even, at one point, separating dresses on hangers and peering behind them.

'Mammy?'

Without hope she searched the kneehole cave beneath her own desk in her bedroom, the curtained space for the gas meter, the recess where the Zimmer stood. God knows what nonsense could get into her mother's head sometimes. She could believe she was sheltering from the Blitz or hiding from a mad axeman or releasing a mouse from a trap. Any excuse. There was one thing that would settle it. She ran up the stairs again and looked at the side of the bed. The old woman's slippers were gone. She went nowhere without them. Last thing, getting into bed, she put her feet together, withdrew from her slippers and swung her legs into bed. Getting up was the reverse. She swung her legs out of bed and inserted her feet into her slippers and stood up. 'Good morning, Vera. Fresh and well you're looking.'

If the noise she'd heard when she first began to run the bath – the floorboard on the landing – if that was the old girl leaving, then she'd had a good start. But not enough of a start to be off the radar. Vera would have a look around the likely places, *then* she would phone the police.

She dressed in jeans and a navy sweater and flung the dressing gown over her bedside chair. A good pair of flat shoes. It was not a cold night, but she put on an anorak in case the rain started again and checked that her keys were in the pocket. She opened the front door and looked out. Still no sign of her.

It had been raining constantly since Thursday but now the pavements were in the process of drying. She sniffed the air and was about to pull the front door shut, but decided to leave it on the push, just in case her mother would come back by some circuitous route and have to sit on the step like an orphan. Burglars could steal what they liked. There was little of value in the house. The last thing any money-grubbing burglar would be interested in was her notebooks. Even she couldn't earn a ha'penny out of them. But they would be about the only thing she would miss. Of course they could take her computer. She'd no idea what was backed up and what was not. That would be serious.

She walked down the short path. A line from the hymn 'Star of the Sea' came to her. 'Pray for the wanderer, pray for me.' The shops – that would be the first place to look. Lily had travelled to these shops, day in, day out, for years. Her feet would take her there.

It was not quite nine o'clock. Around the horizon there were dark clouds. Behind them, just visible, a moon. Lights in houses were beginning to come on – too early for bedrooms – but downstairs lights, kitchen lights. In some dark rooms there was the flicker of television. A man crossed a bright window, a woman paused before pulling curtains. Glimpses. Like small film clips.

But why did the woman pause? What was in the curtain-puller's mind? Maybe she was thinking, who is that woman walking in the street – where is she going at this time on a Sunday night? Maybe a woman like that wouldn't be interested in those kind of questions – it might never occur to her to put herself in someone else's shoes.

But nosiness was such a human thing. Vera's mother hadn't much time for it. 'It's none of your business,' she'd say. 'Keep your neb out of it – it has nothing to do with you.' Without curiosity, science wouldn't exist. Neither would there be any writing. No *Anna Karenina*, no *Middlemarch*. These electric-light fragments of other people's lives underlined how depressingly alike we all were. That could be me, Vera thought. Pausing and pulling. A Cinderella doll, maybe. She knew that most people led lives as vivid and complex as her own. But . . . That woman, for instance, could be having an affair – and the pause is giving a signal to her lover as he waits in his car beneath the shadow of the trees. Or maybe she has a baby crying in the back room. *Nobody* has affairs when they have a baby in the back room. Nobody writes with a pram in the hall. There's no bloody time. Who was it said that? Definitely a male writer. But it was more complex than that. Her friends – other teachers – had said you'd no idea what exhaustion was like until you'd had a baby.

'You don't know my third-years.'

On the other hand, maybe that woman pulling the curtains was giving herself something to do. To avoid giving in to the crying baby. The pause was an attempt to prolong the process. She's telling herself there has to be an instant when the child stops crying and falls asleep by itself.

Blackbirds were singing loudly. At different distances, but all within earshot. One flew across a garden at head height and came to rest on a fence post. That upward tilt of the tail, on landing. Magpies chattered as if a cat was about. The moon was slightly more than a half moon. The first time she'd heard it called 'gibbous' she'd been driven to the dictionary.

There were no people on the road. Of that she was glad. She didn't fancy answering questions.

'Off somewhere nice?'

'No, my Holy Grail is my crazy mother.'

People's gardens looked their best at this time of year. Vivid with flowers, the air alive with green smells. And brown ones too. Soil, roots, damp undergrowth. The body-odour of bushes. All that recent rain flushing out the smells. Distantly she heard a baby crying – a tiny baby. Maybe she'd been right about the woman pulling the curtains.

She turned the corner and heard traffic on the main road. There was a group of teenagers gathered around a lamp post – some on bikes. Before she came level with them, the street lights came on – a bright scarlet. She was aware of baseball caps, white sneakers, miniskirts. They were laughing and screaming. One sat on his saddle with his feet on the handlebars, showing off.

Vera went over. 'Did you see an old woman going past here?'

'Naw,' said a girl in a cropped T-shirt.

'Wearing slippers.'

The boy on the bike shook his head.

'Sorry, Missus.'

The light above was gradually changing its colour. Losing its red, becoming sodium yellow, turning to bright.

The shops served the local community – a newsagent, hairdresser's, wine merchant, a fish-and-chip shop. Some people in the chippie were waiting for their orders to be made up. On a Sunday evening, for God's sake? She didn't go into the newsagent's, but looked between the advertising postcards stuck to the window and saw it was empty. Big Mary, who worked there, would have known what to do and phoned long ago if Lily had turned up. Would her mother be in her nightdress? Or would she have dressed herself, as if going out somewhere? The thought had not occurred to her before – she hadn't checked if there was anything missing from her wardrobe or the hallstand. God forbid, maybe she was naked – kicked the nightdress under the bed. I'm just off for a shower. This was all she needed. Vera still had work to do.

She came to the hairdresser's. The place was in darkness, the drying hoods and chairs were faintly luminous at the back of the shop, like something from a science-fiction film. On a table at the window, lit by street lights, a pile of magazines. The gorgeous smell of chips and vinegar wafted past her. Big Mary had come to the door to lock up. She was smoking a cigarette.

'I suppose you haven't seen Lily?'

'Aw, Vera, she's not away again, is she?' Mary put the cigarette in her mouth and pulled down the metal door shutter with all her might. The sound was awful, like a train derailment. 'Sorry about the noise. When did you last see her?'

'She was tucked up in her bed about an hour ago.'

'You never know, do you?'

Big Mary had a great way with her. Her sympathy was obvious, the way she tilted her head to one side and made a clucking noise with her tongue.

'What about the police? Have you phoned them?'

'It's too early to make a fuss,' said Vera. 'I haven't looked in all the likely places yet.'

'Say a wee prayer to St Francis. He'll find her for you,' said Mary. 'I would stay and give you a hand to look, but . . . '

'I'm sure you want to go home.'

Big Mary pulled a face of apology and said, 'Actually I have somebody waiting for me. I've my own mess to clear . . . '

'Away you go,' said Vera.

Big Mary waved and eased herself into her car. She rolled the window down as she drove off and threw out her cigarette. It sparked off the roadway.

'I'll keep an eye out for her,' she shouted.

Not knowing what to do next, Vera stood looking down at the pavement. Chewing gum, stuck all over the black asphalt, looked like stars in the night sky. So many wads, it was hard to believe. In school the kids knew not to spit it out, but they did, and the school jannie had to take a high-powered hose to the yard.

The thought of school drained her. Tomorrow morning. A double period with that dreadful class of boys. The sooner teaching was all over, the better. She had hopes for a retirement package within a couple of years – had discussed it informally with the Assistant Head. Then she could sub wherever she liked. And the money was so much better. But the main thing was that she could do what she wanted with her own time. Her hobby would become the thing. She would write her book.

Another side-effect was that she wouldn't have to leave her mother on her own all day. When Vera was at school she rang every lunchtime and checked everything was okay – that her mother was making herself something to eat. God knows how the old woman put in her day. She'd given up reading a paper ages ago. The only thing she'd watch on TV was *Countdown*. Her one task was to have the potatoes boiling for Vera coming in from school. Before going out in the morning Vera would have them peeled and in salted water on the cooker – all her mother had to do was to switch on the gas. That was the way they did it, since Lily had thrown a potato and smashed the kitchen window.

'What were you thinking of?'

'I was saving myself a walk each time.'

'What are you talking about?'

'The spuds are in the veggie rack. And the sink's over there.' The old woman pointed as if Vera would not understand. 'So to save myself a walk every time, I was firing them into the sink.' She started to laugh. 'But I fired one too hard. Through the bloody windae.'

Breaking the window wasn't the worst. One day, coming in from school, Vera had noticed a smell of gas. She'd let a yell out of her and dashed to the kitchen. Whatever the old woman had done, the place was filling up, getting ready to explode. She flung every window open, flapped a towel to clear the air and, at the same time, tackled her mother, 'What in the name of God did you do?'

'I dunno.' Her mother was groggy and half asleep in her armchair.

'You *must* know, Mammy,' shouted Vera, 'if we're going to stop it happening again.' The old woman wrinkled up her face. 'We could all have been blown to smithereens. In future I'll turn on the spuds when I come in. Then we can sit and twiddle our thumbs for the best part of an hour waiting for the dinner.'

Then her mother cried because she'd been scolded. Vera plucked some tissues from a box and handed them to her, ended up apologising and hugging her, patting her stooped back.

She crossed the road away from the shops and took a right turn down towards the river. The church was the next best place to look. It was beginning to get dark now – moving from dusk to night. She could see the length of the tree-lined avenue in the street lights. A fox trotted into the middle of the road and looked both ways, cheeky as you like. Vera stopped and stood motionless until it moved off again. Then another appeared. A pair of them. In the street light they looked grey. Amazing to see them like that. Living *in* the city, but not *of* it. Wild. Like Ted Hughes' 'The Thought Fox', which she taught fifth-years. A reality on the street, like a sentence completed on a page. It was hard to imagine it was these creatures who made the terrifying noises she'd heard some nights behind their house – like someone being tortured – shrieks and screams. Or strangling babies. A neighbour told her it was the foxes. Fighting among themselves. Or having sex.

In the summer dark the church loomed grey – as D. H. Lawrence would say, 'like an upturned boat'. Its doors were shut. The grounds were silent except for the faint hush of water from the back of the building. There was a shortcut from the upper road, down a steep slope and across a concrete footbridge. She walked around the outside of the church, looking this way and that. The moon reflected jumpily on the irregular panes of the dark stained-glass windows. When she rounded the corner, the roar of the water became louder. All natural water journeys are to the sea. Just as birth is a start and death is an end. She went to look across the bridge. The overhanging trees made it dark. Restless shadows. She didn't like the look of this spot at this time. Too spooky by half. In daylight it was pleasant. Milton's chequered shade. Once she'd seen altar boys, in their vestments, sneaking a smoke here. There was something pale in the middle of the bridge. She went closer, shaded her eyes with an arched hand. The paleness moved. It was her. Her mother in her night-dress, with her shock of white hair. Two ugly sisters rolled into one. Standing looking over the bridge. Vera was going to call out, but was afraid of startling her. Causing her to do something daft. It would be the simplest thing in the world for a wandering, distracted old woman to make a mistake and end up in the river. Vera thought about that. The slightest tip on the back, an accidental nudge with her shoulder. A fright. The old woman would know nothing about it. An inquest would hear that Vera had been out looking, doing her very best to find her mother. Big Mary would give evidence. And so would those kids on bicycles. Her head was away ahead of her. Making stories.

She moved closer to the bridge. With all the recent rain, the water was loud. She spoke quietly so as not to startle her too much.

'Mammy.'

Then louder.

'Mammy.'

The old woman stood with her elbows on the balustrade, staring down into the water. She was wearing her pale-blue nightie and her carpet slippers. 'Lily.' At her name, the old woman turned. She creased her eyes, trying to see in the gloom. 'Who's that? Vera?'

'Who else?'

'What on earth are you doing out here?'

'Looking for you. Come on. I've to get up in the morning.'

'What time is it?'

Vera turned on her heel. 'Late,' she said. 'Come on.' Then she put her fist on her hip and made a cup handle of her arm. The old woman began to chin-shiver.

'Wait a minute.' Lily summoned up a spit and dropped it, disappearing into the darkness below.

'Hook on,' said Vera. Her mother took her arm and they walked past the church, the old woman at her own pace, she at the old woman's. On the roadway, at each step, her slippers trailed against the tarmac – making a noise.

'I was going to say a mouthful of prayers,' said Lily, 'but the church was closed. Why would that be?'

'The sacristan needs to his bed.'

Her mother seemed not to hear, or else she took no heed. She said, 'Mammy called in earlier on.'

'Did she now?'

'Looking well, too, she was.'

'Your mother must be a right age these days?'

'Talking about there being no money. Again.'

'You're beginning to wander, Mother. I dunno what you're talking about half the time.'

'She lives a life of fear, that woman.' Lily held onto her arm more tightly. Vera felt the shivering in her mother's grip. 'Says I to her – I can't lend you anything. The cupboard's bare, as far as I'm concerned.'

'I know what you mean,' Vera said, looking both ways before crossing the road.

'I'm glad you don't have any worries like that about me.'

'Aye. Nothing to worry about, apart from breaking windows and blowing up the house. And pounding the streets in your nightie. Come on, I've my work in the morning. And me a world-class worrier at the best of times.'

As they were approaching the house Mr Kincaid, next door but one, was setting out with his walking stick.

'Evening,' said Vera.

'Showery enough,' said Mr Kincaid.

In the name of God, thought Vera, aren't some people weird? Here I am, out walking with an eighty-four-year-old woman in her nightdress and slippers and all he can do is talk about the weather. Swinging his silver stick. Christ Almighty! Taking it for a walk because he has no dog.

The door was still on the push. The burglars were having a night off. It didn't matter if she had stuff that wasn't backed up. Vera helped her mother onto the step.

'Straight to bed now,' she said. 'You'll be exhausted.'

'Divil the bit of me,' snapped Lily. 'I could walk there and back again.'

'What has you so restless?'

'I dunno. I could put my legs in the fridge.'

'Don't be daft.'

'I'm not ready for bed yet.'

'You'll do as you're told.'

They climbed the stairs with Vera taking up the rear, her hands up and at the ready – just in case the oul girl should fall backwards. Lily went into the toilet.

'Leave the door open,' said Vera. As she waited she looked for the millionth time at the Pope's blessing of Lily's marriage. Pope Pius XII, his white skullcap, his aquiline nose, his gold-rimmed spectacles. At the fake calligraphic script, making out it was old and therefore more valid. And holier – if there was such a word. Vera went downstairs and came back with all the night stuff, including a bottle of Jameson. Lily flushed the toilet. She washed and dried her hands and came out, smoothing them down her brushed-cotton nightdress.

'Into bed now, and not a word outta you.'

The old woman ambled into her room and did as she was told.

'I was going to give you your Mogadon after I finished my bath. But, oh no – the bird had flown?' Vera pushed the sleeping pill from its blister pack and set it on the dressing table beside the carafe of water and its glass. 'Out galloping the countryside. I'll give you something to put a stop to your galloping.'

Lily saw the whiskey bottle.

'Am I getting a wee treat?'

'Not that you deserve it – after tonight's performance.' Vera unscrewed the top and poured a substantial glass, which she handed to Lily. Then she turned and picked up the carafe of water. As if she didn't know, she said, 'Say when.'

'Right up,' said the old woman. Vera poured and the colour of the whiskey lightened, became straw-coloured to the rim. 'Will you not join me?'

'Naw – I've work to do.' She gave her the sleeping pill into the palm of her hand, pressed it, so it would not spring out and get lost in the bedclothes, as it had many times before. Lily brought her hand to her mouth and set the pill on her tongue. She held the glass up as if to say cheers, but the word got distorted because of the impediment of the pill. She flushed it down with whiskey and smacked her lips.

'Take it easy,' said Vera. 'I don't want it to go with your breath.' Vera tidied the pillows behind her back. 'Is that okay for you?'

The old woman nodded.

'You'd wonder that she would still be afraid – at her age.'

'What?'

'Of being left without any money.'

Lily drank off the rest of the whiskey and smiled expectantly at Vera, who was looking at her watch.

'One for the road?' the old woman said.

Vera poured her another glass and sat on the bedside chair while her mother eased back into her pillows.

'Are you sure you'll not join me?'

Vera hesitated. 'Maybe to celebrate finding you.'

'Don't be so sarcastic.'

Vera went downstairs for a clean glass.

'Thank God tomorrow's Friday,' Lily said when her daughter came back into the bedroom.

'It's Monday,' said Vera.

When all this started – a good few years ago – Vera had said to her, 'Mammy, I think you're beginning to dote.'

Her mother had stared back at her for some time.

'You think I don't know?'

The old woman had cried silently and for a long time that day. Vera never mentioned it again.

Now she poured herself a Jameson and diluted it.

'Well cheers, Mammy.' They clinked glasses. Lily raised the glass shakily and drank some of it. She looked around the room as if it was new to her.

'What's that?'

'What?'

'Shining in the corner.'

Vera turned and looked. 'Where's your television glasses?'

'God only knows.'

'It's your Zimmer frame.'

'What's that?'

'After your fall. To help you walk.'

'Naw – I don't mind that.'

'We never gave it back to the hospital. You kept saying it'd come in useful.'

After a while Vera raised her glass again.

'Cheers.'

'Oh, I didn't hear you, love.' And they clinked again. And drank again. There was a long silence.

Vera said, 'I'd some nice news on Friday.'

'What was that?'

'I'm going to have a story published in the *Independent*. I got word on Friday.'

'Are you going to work for them?'

'Noooo, they have a New Writing page. It'll be a one-off. A story.'

'Oh.'

Her mother sipped from her glass noisily, tried to narrow her eyes to better see her daughter.

'But you're not leaving the teaching?'

'No.'

'The money's gotta come in from somewhere,' said the old woman.

'Oh, they'll pay a bit. Not much, mind you. It's far more important to get your name recognised. To have readers. Nobody does it for the pittance they pay.'

'I know what you mean.'

How foolish, thought Vera. Here she was trying to talk to her mother about something she held precious. Her mother, who'd barely read a book in her life. Even a couple of years ago she'd had difficulty following a story on television. At a crucial moment in the film they were watching, Lily would stand and say, 'Well, that's me off to bed.' Now she no longer tried to follow stuff on television. This was the same woman Vera was talking to about getting a story published. She was trying to have a literary conversation with a woman in her dotage. She looked at her mother. She seemed to be getting smaller, slipping down the pillows.

'That sleeping pill's making me feel woozy,' she said.

The old woman drank off the rest of the whiskey and handed Vera the glass. In the same motion she slid down the bed, sighed and turned her shoulder into the pillow.

Vera went to the window and opened it a fraction to let some air circulate. Might help her mother avoid a cloth-mouth in the morning after all that whiskey. She became aware of the honeysuckle from next door. The smell stronger, sweeter at night. She heard Mr Kincaid, returning from his walk, twirling and tapping his stick. He looked up at her briefly. Probably saw Vera the way she'd glimpsed the woman earlier, pulling curtains. A tiny onscreen trailer. She found it difficult to believe Mr Kincaid thought anything about her or her mother. Men. Could he imagine anything of the life that was going on two doors up from him? He would have no insight, could never deduce what had just happened between her and her mother. Was a Zimmer frame in the attic any worse than a pram in the hall? Vera tugged the curtains tightly together in order to keep out the light that would come in the morning. She turned to the bed, pulled the clothes up around the old woman's neck and, patting her on the back, said goodnight, even though she was just beginning to snore.

BLANK PAGES

The storm was there when he woke, growling away, but not yet off the leash. The newspaper had been shoved through the letter box and had landed inside the outer storm doors. When he lifted it, it was damp and soundless. The cat mewed at his feet and rubbed against his legs as he padded about in his slippers and dressing gown. He shook some dry, tinkling cat food into the empty bowl but the cat did not move to it as she usually did. She stood staring. Then he half filled another dish beside it with milk. There were yellowed rings crusted around the inside of the dish. The cat didn't seem to take any notice. Now she purred and continued this way and that against his legs. What was the word Joyce used in *Ulysses*? How did he spell it? There was an M and a K and AIOW. He opened the middle pages of the newspaper to try and tent them over the radiator to dry. He prepared his breakfast – porridge made in the microwave, a slice of wheaten bread with crab-apple jelly, a cup of black Earl Grey tea. He carried it all with care to the gloom of the front room. Mkaiow – that was it. That was Joyce's word for cat-speak. But he should check it.

He sat in his armchair by the window overlooking the street and ate without reading. The sky was slate-coloured, the trees in the Gardens opposite rocked to and fro and their branches thrashed about. 'There was no possibility of taking a walk that day.' The rain was too much for the gratings along the side of the road and it ran as a river down the middle of the street, where no river had run before. Beneath the large trees the downpour seemed to leap back off the black tarmac. Not only the rain pelting down past his window, but cascades from the tenement guttering. He could barely see out because of the drops adhering to the glass. They shivered in the gusts and distorted what was beyond. The wind roared and buffeted in the chimney.

He could not remember a red-alert weather warning before. Was this a new thing? Global warming? He knew about the Beaufort Scale, but that was a long time ago in secondary-school Geography. The traffic-light system seemed an innovation. Yellow for watch out, amber for warning. The TV weather girl the previous night said it would get much worse as the day went on. Eleven o'clock and after. That was the danger time, she'd said. The red alert. She seemed to enjoy the impending disaster – grinning, pointing, pacing back and forth in front of the camera. She and the male newsreader seemed to have a bond. Because it was about the weather, they could relax and joke, be unscripted for a few moments. It was not political. There were no sides. Balance was not necessary. Weather was weather. She wore things to show her figure to advantage – but not lewd, not libidinous. The TV people would never allow it.

His wife, Kathy, had died two years ago and he missed her so much. Occasionally he still talked to her. She'd had a fair warning that the worst was going to happen and had prepared for it. She was the one who was the manager, the administrator. Box files stood on the study shelf, clearly labelled for him in black felt tip – PENSIONS, TAX, HOUSE, ROYALTIES, BANK, and so on. She'd prepared and simplified them, so as he could work her system. Then her illness had slowed her down and she'd ceased to care. She left things behind her – like her clothes. And the cat. And silence.

He reached down and scratched his ankle through his sock. The cat followed him into the front room and stood there. Normally she sprang into the empty armchair opposite him.

'Not yourself today, eh?'

She looked at him and sat down on the carpet, began grooming herself. She gave up and tucked her paws in beneath her.

'Comfy? Maybe get some work done today,' he said. 'As long as you don't keep me back.'

For ages after Kathy died the cat was in mourning. She knew there was something very wrong. A place was missing and the man was no substitute. She wouldn't come near him. Then recently, to his surprise, she would occasionally pad in and leap up onto his lap for the evening. Purring. Then it wouldn't happen again for weeks.

She was a tabby, striped and yellow-eyed. He'd grown up with cats as a child. They weren't *his* cats, but were of his mother's choosing. Of course he played with them, had considered them *his* pets. It seemed natural that this present one and he should be companions.

He finished eating. His cup of tea was still half full. He remembered the cupcakes in the Tupperware box. At this time of the day he shouldn't, but when there was nobody to stop him . . . He shrugged and heaved himself out of the chair, went to the kitchen and came back with a cupcake – with icing and coloured sprinkles on top. There was only one more left. When he passed the newspaper on the radiator he saw that it was still grey, still too wet to read.

He eased the bun from its fluted paper and ate it, drinking the remainder of his tea. The local newspaper was no great loss. Every morning he subedited rather than read the paper. Misprints, misspellings, misattributions. Photographs with the wrong captions. Grammar glitches. When he found one, he would hoot out loud and the cat would look at him. In days gone by, he would have shown them to his wife. It was just penny-pinching by the paper's owners – making do with fewer subeditors. 'Let readers work it out for themselves.'

The cat raised her head and looked at him. Buns for breakfast? she seemed to say. He opened yesterday's paper and read the bits he had skipped. Then realised why he had skipped them. He skimmed the headlines rather than read the columns. Looked at the cartoons. Sometimes he did not understand them, but when this happened he blamed the cartoonist – not himself. Turning the newspaper pages, he accidentally brushed the bun paper from the table to the floor. He couldn't be bothered to pick it up.

'Later,' he said to the cat. She moved to investigate what had come down from above. The letters page was full of its usual pomposities and smart clichés – no better for being read a day later. Even on the second day the business section was of no interest to him. He heard this strange noise – rasp, rasp, rasp. And he looked and there was the cat licking the inside of the bun paper. And as she licked, the paper moved a little. She hadn't the brains to put her foot on it, to steady it, to hold it still. So she pushed it round the room with her little sandpaper tongue.

'Like the sweetness? Eh, puss?' He scratched his ankle by gathering the material of his sock between his fingertips and moving it up and down over the itchy place. Then the same with the other ankle. It was a delicious sensation. Scratching with fingernails drew blood and was to be avoided.

Standing up was becoming an increasingly difficult manoeuvre. He helped himself forward from the armchair with a rocking motion, removed his cup and plate to the kitchen, where he washed them and stood them in the empty draining rack. That way he didn't allow the place to become a midden. He went back into the front room and picked the bun paper off the floor. The cat had licked it clean, her tongue had ironed out the fluted nature of the paper. He dropped it into the wastepaper basket.

An email from his publisher had to be answered. Also one from his agent. He went to the study, sat down and tapped the keyboard into life. While he was typing he noticed he had not trimmed his fingernails for some time. After he pressed 'send' he sat staring at the screen. He'd used a picture of Capri as his desktop image, one he'd taken himself – the islands ghostly on the sea's horizon, barely visible. It was useless as a photograph, but the items on the desktop stood out starkly. It was the last time they'd been on holiday together.

He got up from the swivel chair and went into the bedroom. He began on his fingernails. Each cut crescent fell into the wastepaper basket with a tick. Cutting the nails of his left hand was straightforward, but he had a different style for doing the right hand. Clumsy snips, guided and angled by his lesser hand. He smoothed off any rough edges with his wife's emery board, which was still in the jug at her side of the bed, then went back into the study.

He had a number of shortcuts to work-in-progress on the screen but none of them seemed to attract him. Then, for no good reason he could think of, he sharpened a pencil. He had a battery-operated pencil sharpener, but it had run out of power and he could never get his act together sufficiently to buy new batteries and fit them just at the moment when he needed a sharp pencil. So he used a small sharpener – like a kid uses at school. As the point turned, a frill of pencil-smelling wood unfurled from it. The point was sharp and perfect. Dangerous even. He kept a box of Staedtler pencils on his desk – not for drawing, but for their cedar smell.

Then he sat staring at the Isle of Capri for almost five minutes. The cat came into the study and purred around his feet.

'The wind has gone out of my sails, Lui,' he said.

The cat was called not after an Irish poet or a French king but after the place it was born. Ardlui near Loch

Lomond. He and his wife had been driving to the west coast for a weekend break all those years ago and had stopped for a coffee at a farm place that sold eggs and fresh vegetables. It was a beautiful warm spring day and, unusually for Scotland, tables had been set outside. As they had their coffee, a child had come out from the kitchen with a basin of porridge and set it in the yard. Cats of all ages and shapes and sizes appeared from nowhere and converged on it. There was a kitten with only a tiny remnant of a tail, which attracted his wife's attention. When they were leaving she got into a cat conversation with the farmer's wife. It was arranged that they would call on their way back and take one home. For no cost whatsoever.

This was the beast now purring around his ankles. With a quarter-tail pointing in the air.

'You're some pup,' he said. The cat ceased purring and stood facing the grey filing cabinet. In the beginning he'd wanted to call her 'Rover', but Kathy wouldn't go along with it. Lui's whiskers brushed the grey metal of the filing cabinet and she stood there for ages. Stock still, as if looking intensely at something infinitesimal. Or immense.

In the hallway on the bookshelf he found his copy of *Ulysses*, the revised Bodley Head of 1960. He flicked through and found the chapter he was looking for. He said, 'Mkgnao!' as best he could. Then lower down the page he saw 'Mrkgnao'. Not quite the same. And harder to say. The page turned almost by itself and he saw another version. 'Mrkrgnao'. Different again. He was standing there, trying to articulate this word, when he heard a key turn in the lock of the front door.

'Hi there,' he said.

He turned to see Teresa coming in. She was carrying a flat Tupperware box with some ironed shirts folded neatly on top. She was trying to shelter them from the rain with her hand.

'What a day.' She shook her hair back into place. 'And it's supposed to be July. Hard to believe we were in a heatwave last week. How's it going?'

'This morning I'm a towering inferno of creativity. In a word, Red Alert.'

'Good to hear it, Frank. But that's two words.'

He gave a little smile and set the book back in its alphabetical place on the shelf.

'I'll put the kettle on,' he said.

'And I'll make the coffee,' she said. She set her bunch of keys and the shirts on the hall sideboard. 'Don't let me forget my keys.'

'Did you get parked?'

'Just round the corner.'

'I feel remarkably lucky when I get a space in my own postcode.'

She carried the Tupperware box into the kitchen. He went to the front room and sat in the armchair by the window. The windowpanes of the house opposite were flexing in the storm. A plastic shopping bag whirled up and disappeared out of sight.

'You shouldn't have ventured out on such a day,' he said when Teresa came in carrying a tray. He took his coffee and a bun. So did she. 'The second today,' he said.

'Oh, Frank – they're supposed to be a treat. Don't let yourself go. They're full of sugar and margarine.'

'Did you bring a fresh supply?'

'I did.'

'Are you trying to get rid of me?' he smiled. 'Naw – you're very good. Your timing is perfect. There was only one left.'

'How's it going, really?' she asked.

He moved his hand in a see-saw motion and pulled a face.

'Are you getting any work done?'

'Yeah, but it's all the wrong kind of work.'

He reached down and scratched his ankle beneath his sock. Teresa saw a wisp of red.

'Stop it,' she said. 'You've drawn blood.'

'That's what writers write with.'

'The more you do it,' she said, 'the worse it gets.'

'Just like writing.'

'I'm talking about scratching.'

'How could I? I've just cut my fingernails.'

'What are we talking about here?'

'The pleasure of scratching an itch.'

'Not writing?'

'No. Very little pleasure in that. Too much like work.' He blew on his coffee and sipped it warily. 'There's a holy man somewhere in India and he spends his time rolling about the roads from Bombay to God-knows-where – well, I'd rather be doing that.'

'You're a terrible man.'

'He has a team to sweep the road in front of him – clear away any stones or broken glass. Or drawing pins.'

'What are you talking about, Frank?'

'This guy, this holy man – I read about him online the other night – instead of walking on pilgrimages, he rolls.

Hundreds and hundreds of miles. Not head over heels but the other way: shoulder over shoulder. Like a rolling pin.'

'How bizarre.'

'People are getting soft. In my day they wouldn't have swept the roads.' Teresa smiled. 'Lui likes your buns too. Licks the inside of the paper.'

'She's a good judge.' She looked around for the cat.

'She's behaving very strangely this morning.'

'Like what?'

'I dunno. Standing staring at things. Like my filing cabinet.'

There was a lull in the conversation as they listened to the wind. Teresa set her cup on the wooden arm of her chair.

'I think I'd better get on with what I came to do.'

Frank nodded.

'It's very good of you.'

'She was *my* friend . . . '

He nodded. These things did not need to be said out loud.

'Let me get dressed first,' he said. 'Before you go in there.'

'So it's anything that Oxfam can make a few quid on – everything else goes in the bin?'

'Correct.'

'I'll put the Oxfam things in the car,' said Teresa, 'and the next time I'm over at the other side of town . . . '

'You're very good,' he said. 'But there's no need to go to that amount of trouble. Just go to the nearest Oxfam. I'd never notice anything of hers.'

'But you're a writer . . . You're supposed to notice.'

'I only notice odd things,' he said. 'Not that I do much rummaging on the women's racks these days. There's black bin bags in the kitchen cupboard.'

Teresa stood and smiled. Frank looked up at her.

'Tasteful of me to get black bin bags,' he said. 'That's the kind of thing I notice.' He reached down and had a scratch at his other ankle. Teresa changed direction. She was down on her knees on the carpet in front of him.

'Let's have a look.'

He rolled his eyes, then showed her his ankles beneath his navy socks. She tightened her lips.

'It's been like that for ages,' he said. 'Some kind of an allergy.'

She looked more closely.

'I think they're bites.'

After he washed and dressed, Frank went back into the study. Teresa had gone into his bedroom and closed the door, leaving the faintest taint of her perfume in the air of the hallway. He was reluctant to face the computer screen again and stood looking through the venetian blinds at the wind cuffing the street. The venetian blinds were Kathy's idea – to give the room the right feeling, like an office in Manhattan, where both of them could work: he at his writing, she at her bookkeeping and various correspondences and 'projects', as she called them. All the other rooms in the house had curtains. He sat down in the swivel chair at his desk. The cat had not moved but was now sitting, still looking at the filing cabinet. He reached out and scratched Lui's head. 'Teresa says it's *you* who's to blame. You and all that hot weather.' It was hard to believe that they had just gone through ten scorching days in June – days of him sitting at the doorway, having to wear sunblock, remembering to make ice cubes, nights when it was too hot to sleep. And now this. The day before yesterday the mare's tails had appeared in the sky, the rain had started and it hadn't given up since.

'*The glass is falling hour by hour, the glass will fall for ever, but if you break the bloody glass, you won't hold up the weather.* One of your better ones, Lui,' he said to the cat. He went to the shelf above his printer. Several packets of white copy paper, the top packet torn open. He slid a sheet out of it.

'No shortage of A4, eh?' He went back into the front room and looked down at the floor. He dropped the sheet of paper on the carpet. In the draught from the door, it hovered a little before settling. Then he retired to the sofa to watch. The carpet was plain – some kind of a cream colour typical of Kathy's taste – but on top of it in front of the fireplace was a large Persian rug: densely patterned, darkly coloured with blacks and maroons and ruby-reds. Hand-knotted, she said, when she bought it. It was on this rug that the white page had come to rest. He watched the white rectangle on and off for maybe half an hour but there was no sign of anything. All that time he could hear faint noises and movement from the bedroom. The wardrobe door squeaking open. Then closing again. The creak of an ironing board.

'The blank page,' he said and heaved himself to his feet. He stood, put on his glasses and stared down, bending his knees slightly to bring the page into focus. Nothing.

Not a single thing. He went back into the study. The cat was still there. He took a handful of sheets from the open packet and riffled them, the way he did before feeding them into the printer. The cat followed him.

In the front room he began to lay the sheets on the floor.

'Carpet bombing,' he said. 'The more there are, the greater the chance.' He straightened a sheet with the toe of his shoe. 'Oh, 'tis far from sheets of white paper I was reared,' he said to the cat.

When he first began writing – some ten or fifteen years after the war – there was a great scarcity of paper. He'd written on the backs of old Christmas cards, school jotters, blank exam booklets, anything he could lay his hands on. In the real olden days, paper was so scarce they used to write over what was written there before. At right-angles – warp and woof.

'Palimpsest,' he told Lui. He allowed another sheet to zigzag to the floor and stooped to straighten it. 'Such extravagance.'

He laid down a sheet by the sofa where Kathy used to sit, or at least where her feet used to rest on the carpet. It covered the dark half moon that had developed, not with dirt, but from compression of the carpet fibres. He lifted the paper sheet and, with the flat of his hand, tried to change the nap of the fibres, to make them paler. To erase her mark.

'Forgive me.'

Then he took up his position on the sofa again, lifting up his feet, shoes and all. His eyes ran along the rows of blank pages. Then down the columns. The carpet was almost completely covered. But it was too early to say.

Indeed, if he had seen anything so soon, he would have been amazed. He looked at his watch. It was well after midday. The storm seemed to have done its worst. The weather lassie on the TV wasn't far wrong. Then he saw a black speck on one of the pages. Was it dirt? Had it just blown there? The storm had filled the air with dust and disturbance. He approached with care, bent over, his hands on his thighs. The black speck disappeared as if by magic.

'Ya bastard.'

He stood crouched in excitement, looking from one page to the other. Where had it gone? Then another speck appeared on a sheet further to his left – over by the fire-place. Was that the same one? Had it just blown there? Or had it jumped? Then another one appeared in the centre.

'The story's beginning to unfold.'

He looked more closely. Was it ragged fluff or were they legs? He made pincers of his finger and thumb and picked up what was on the centre page. It was so easy. It required no stealth whatsoever. Unlike pursuing a fly. But what could he do with it? He carried it like a pinch of snuff to the bathroom, plugged and filled the washbasin. Then immersed his fingers and parted them underwater. The black speck revolved in the current. Frank made a fist and shook it at the speck, but did not go as far as punching the air. He bent for a closer look against the white porcelain. It was more brown than black. It had appendages, too small to distinguish without his glasses.

He went into the hall and walked quickly to his bedroom. For some reason he knocked.

'Come in.'

Frank looked around. The wardrobe doors were wide open. Teresa was holding up a dress still on its coat-hanger. The smell in the room was faint but it was more Kathy's than Teresa's. She had set up the ironing board and there was a little folded pile of his wife's underwear on the bedside table. He said, 'If there's anything you want to keep for yourself?'

She shook her head vigorously.

'We were friends. I couldn't,' she said. 'Maybe a couple of scarves. She was very good with scarves.'

'Whatever you like. I promise I won't be reminded.' She raised the dress to her chin and looked at herself in the full-length mirror.

'I don't want to remind you of anybody,' she said. 'I want you to think of me as me.'

'Come and see this,' he said.

'What?' She let the dress slide from its hanger into the open mouth of a black bag on the floor.

'Come till you see,' he said. She passed him on her way out. Frank stood looking at the scene in the bedroom.

'Come on,' she said. 'This is no place for you.'

'It's *my* room.'

She lightly pulled him by the arm and he came with her. He led her to the bathroom and pointed into the basin. She stooped and parted her hair, holding it back with both hands.

'You see, I was right,' she said. 'Where did you get it?'

'On one of the paper sheets.'

Teresa bustled past him into the front room where he had placed the sheets on the floor.

'Safety in numbers, Frank. I suggested one sheet and you've covered the place.'

'There's no shortage of blank A4 in this house.'

Still she was holding her hair out of her face as she bent over to examine the pages.

'There you are. And there,' she said, pointing.

'Why do cats never need a haircut?'

'It's the way things are,' she said. 'Look, there's another. That's three. In such a short space of time. I'd have that cat treated, if I was you. Take her to the vet's.'

Frank shook his head.

'There must be millions in that carpet,' he said.

'You'll also need to get someone in. Pest control. Where's the culprit?'

'In the study.'

Teresa walked to the study and Frank followed her. The cat had gone back to standing with her nose almost flat against the bottom drawer of the filing cabinet.

'Is there any fish stored in that drawer?'

'If there is, it'll be under F,' said Frank. 'Very odd, isn't it?'

Teresa crouched and began to scratch the cat's head.

'It's like she's gone blind,' she said. She gently pushed the cat to see if there would be a response. A little stagger was all. 'I don't like the look of this,' said Teresa. 'I'd take her to the vet's and get her checked out, if I was you. Have you got a cat basket?'

'Of course.' But Frank did not move.

'By that time I'll have finished here,' said Teresa. 'Ask the vet about the fleas, as well.'

'That's making a fuss,' said Frank. 'I could maybe get an answer as to why cats never need a haircut.'

*

The only place that smelled worse than the vet's surgery was the cheese shop further down the road. Frank sat with the cat basket on his knee, trying not to breathe. Occasionally he leaned down to see into the cage and mutter calming words. Then saw himself from the cat's point of view – looming. He remembered once, on one of the cat's night outings, she'd caught a mouse and presented it for them to see on the front door step. It lay stone-dead on its side, its pale underparts showing in the porch light. Kathy, who'd discovered it, wanted nothing to do with the poor thing. He had to come, armed with a brush, to sweep it with one quick twitch into the gutter. He sat imagining being pounced on by something twenty times your own size. And then, whatever it was, playing with you, toying with you.

There was another woman – middle-aged – also with a cat basket, who kept up a whispered dialogue with her animal. She sat by the doorway. Difficult to tell if her cat had been seen or not. The door to the vet's surgery opened and the girl who had checked him in nodded. He rose and carried the cat basket in front of him at chest height. There was a plaintive mewing from within. He tried to say something comforting but unsentimental. He felt onstage in front of the middle-aged woman.

The vet took his cat from the basket as if it was a simple job. She spoke in a soothing voice.

'What's her name?' she said.

'Lui.'

'Poor Louis,' she said. She stood the cat on the operating table and began stroking her with both hands. First the right hand on the head and down the back, then the left. What remained of the cat's tail came up each time.

'She was acting kinda crazy . . . ' said Frank.

'Like what?'

'Just standing there. Facing the filing cabinet – her nose an inch away from it.'

'Anything else?'

'Bumping into the furniture. Staggering a bit.'

The vet's mouth tightened.

'I don't like the sound of that,' she said.

'Yeah, she's a poor oul thing at the minute . . . '

'You've had her a long time?'

'Seventeen – eighteen years.'

'I remember your wife used to come in with her occasionally. And I remember the missing tail.'

'My wife died. Two years ago.'

'I'm sorry to hear that.'

Her hands were feeling about the cat's body. Looking for something, but disguised as affectionate stroking. The examination continued in silence for a while. The vet looked in the cat's mouth, her eyes, in her ears.

'I can see she's been well treated – well loved. But . . . ' Her voice faltered.

'We discovered fleas,' said Frank. 'That must take it out of them badly.'

The vet nodded and went on stroking. She went back occasionally over areas she had covered.

'If her health had been better, we could have dealt with the flea infestation. But – what with her age and everything . . . '

He opened the door and set the empty cat basket in the hallway. The top was covered with rain. Teresa had set a line of black plastic bags by the doorway. She put her head out of the bathroom.

'Frank – hi.'

He went into the bedroom and took a clean hanky from his bedside drawer.

'Could you carry some of those bags to the car for me,' she called. 'I don't want a bad back tomorrow.' She handed him her car keys. He finished blowing his nose, took the keys and picked up several of the bags and swung them over his shoulder.

When he came back she had her outdoor coat on.

'Has it calmed down anything?' she asked.

'Not much. Maybe a bit.'

'And where's the cat? Are they going to keep her in?'

Frank walked slowly to the front room and indicated with a nod of his head for her to follow. He sidestepped the papers still on the floor and sat down in the armchair.

'I'd forgotten about these,' said Teresa. 'What a midden!'

'Never mind,' said Frank.

Teresa sat at the end of the sofa, her feet resting on the dark patch he'd tried to smooth away earlier. She looked across at him and waited.

'I've had the cat put down,' he said. 'The vet didn't seem to think there was any other option.'

'Aw, Frank. How awful. The poor oul thing.'

'She said it had cat AIDS. Or some other set of letters.'

'I've heard of that.'

Frank shrugged his shoulders. 'She could have had it for years, it seems. I had to make a decision – there and then. I thought, what would Kathy do?'

'You poor man.'

'I liked Lui but I wasn't mad about her, like Kathy was. I talked to her. That was enough.'

'Kathy or the cat?'

He smiled at her joke.

A particularly loud gusting of wind rushed at the window and one of the A4 sheets lifted off the floor, hovered and settled again.

'Did you see that?' said Frank.

'What?'

'The way that sheet rose up. When I was putting them down, I felt a draught coming from the plug socket. Can you believe that? First time I ever felt a three-pronged draught. Wind power from electricity.'

'Frank, what are you talking about?'

He shrugged again and they both became silent.

He cleared his throat and said, 'I'm feeling very low. I don't even want to write about this. Or anything else.' He looked down at the cushion and picked up a cat hair between his finger and thumb. 'Unmistakeable. Each hair has three colours. Black, brown, yellow. Hemingway was a great man for cats. So was Joyce.'

'The writing comes and goes,' she said. 'Hasn't it always?'

'I suppose so.'

There was a long silence. Then Frank said, 'I cried in the car on the way home. When I looked in the mirror and saw the empty basket on the back seat.'

Teresa got up from the sofa and went to him. She sat awkwardly on the arm of the chair and put her arm around his shoulder. Her hand patted him softly. He felt he was fourteen years of age again, wanted to say something to her, but the saying of it could destroy everything, could make her turn on her heel and walk out. The saying of it could provoke scorn, a verbal slap, a how-dare-you. And yet there was the faintest possibility that she might smile, might give it some thought, might even agree.

'Why do you continue to come round?' he said.

'For Kathy's sake,' she said. She gave his shoulder a final squeeze and stood. 'It's just part of the way things are. I'll see you next week.'

And she was away, slamming the front door after her. He sat surrounded by empty pages, examining the tricoloured cat hair. He looked up. Outside the window, the trees seemed less agitated and the roar of the chimney had ceased. Gradually over the evening the silence flowed back into the flat – more obvious now that the cat was no longer there.

SOUNDS AND SWEET AIRS

On the boat train the elderly couple sat opposite, she facing the direction of travel, he with his back to it. The window was covered in raindrops, which moved according to the speed of the train. They entered a tunnel and for a moment everything went dark. When the train emerged they both kept an eye on the weather by watching the tops of trees.

'I don't like the look of it,' he said.

'It'll be okay,' said the woman. 'Nowadays they have those things they put out sideways to calm everything down.'

'Their hands?'

'No. I've forgotten what they're called.'

After a while he spoke again.

'I'm seeing stuff now I never knew existed. Look at that.'

He nodded at the Priority Seats – the purple fabric was patterned with small, stylised figures: a green man with a white stick, a pink girl with a baby, a blue pregnant woman, an orange man with his leg in a plaster.

'What I like is that some people sat down and figured all this out,' said the woman. 'A committee. Who were kind.'

Her partner thought about this.

'But they're all temporary conditions,' he said. 'How do you show depression? Or cancer?'

They checked in at the ferry terminal. A man in uniform behind the desk took their tickets, looked up and confirmed that their first names were Sean and Grace – and issued them with boarding passes.

'They're trying to be an airport, if you ask me,' said Sean. 'Security and X-rays, bloody baggage roundabouts.'

They had no need to check in their luggage. Sean had only a pull-case, Grace carried a cloth bag for essentials. They sat in a row of plastic chairs and looked about them. A young woman in a wheelchair was pushed past and parked at the end of the row opposite. She was wearing jeans and cowboy boots and was making a call on her mobile. Sean noticed that when she finished she slid her mobile into her boot, like it was a holster. Another woman and her toddler came by. The tiny girl spilled her crisps on the wooden floor. The mother, two steps behind her, stopped and waited. The child, with finger and thumb, began to pick each crisp off the floor and eat it.

'She's building up her immunity,' said the mother to Sean. The child then got down on all fours to eat directly off the floor. 'She's been watching the dog.' The mother lifted the child and returned to her seat, laughing.

A third girl appeared. She had a fat rucksack on her back and was wheeling what could only be a harp in a black cover. Sean nudged his wife's elbow.

'Would you look at me?' he said. 'It just so happens I've brought my harp.'

'Leave her alone. What harm has she done you?'

He pointed at his eye.

'Since my operation I can see through people.'

It was a long distance to the boat. Several staircases to get to the correct level, corridors from the terminal that seemed miles long and sloped acutely upwards. So much so that there were little stopping places, upended seats attached to the wall, which said, 'Have a rest.'

'I daren't sit down,' said Grace. 'That would give the game away.'

She was panting between words.

'Hang on and take it easy.' Her husband offered his arm and, when she took it, he clamped onto it. 'I'll go a bit slower. One step at a time.'

As if to predict what the journey held for them, every so often there were little clusters of motion-sickness bags hanging on the wall. They made rustling noises as he plucked out a few and stuffed them in his pocket.

'Single-use plastic,' he said and she smiled.

'Stabilisers.'

'What?'

'The word I couldn't remember. To stop the ship rolling. Stabilisers. Like the side wheels that wee ones have on their bikes.'

'I have to find a purser. First thing. It's all a bit embarrassing.'

On board they were greeted by a uniformed man – white shirt, black company epaulettes. Sean approached him and told him the story of his recent cataract operation and the need to keep his eye-drops cold in the fridge. The purser nodded. Sean squinted down at his watch.

'I'll need them in an hour or so.'

'Just ask at the desk,' said the purser.

'Amidships,' said Sean. 'That's where we want to be – the area of least movement. Up or down, left or right.'

They came to the Quiet Lounge and found an empty corner and sat down. Grace spread their stuff out a bit to give them more room. Outside the wind was whistling and ropes were clacking. A flag fluttered straight out from its flagpole.

'Well, at least there's no muzak,' said Sean. He twisted his head round and checked the window. 'Look at the white horses,' he said. 'And we're still in the harbour.'

'Don't be daft.'

The girl pushing her harp came past and looked at them. She swung the thing round and went back the way she'd come – looking from side to side for a suitable place.

'We're not to her taste,' said Sean.

People came into the lounge and began to sit at tables. They were the ones with cars, because they had no overcoats. One man noisily dumped his big bunch of keys on the table next to Sean and Grace and sat down with his elderly family. One of the old women with him had a conspicuous hearing aid.

'It's filling up,' the driver said loudly to no one in particular.

Grace made a motion to answer the man but Sean pulled a face of caution. And she knew that she shouldn't make a commitment to a conversation so early. For a two-hour sailing. Just in case. Be wary. So she joined her hands and peered down at the table with its raised rim.

'Did you sleep well last night?' Sean said, to draw her away from the family.

'No. You know I never sleep well when I'm away.'

'Why don't you lie down here,' he said. 'Have a bit of a snooze.'

'People are still coming on. It would look lovely with an oul doll like me stretched my length across two or three seats.'

More and more people came in and occupied tables. Like Sean and Grace, they all tried to take more space than they needed in order to keep others at a distance. Arm's length seemed to be too near.

The ferry gradually began to move. The cityscape drifted past, became the grey hills in the distance.

'This reminds me,' Sean leaned over to his wife, 'of one Christmas, when I was about eight, my mother took me down town to see Santa in his grotto. It was supposed to be a train inside the Co-op going to Lapland, but I could see a man winding scenery past a fake window. It was a paper scroll with trees painted on it.' He enacted laborious winding with both hands. 'Not only was Santa a con trick, but so was getting to see him.'

'And you've never been right since,' said Grace. 'You told me that before.'

'I wonder is it still happening.' He closed one eye and nodded towards the window and the glide past of sky and buildings. 'The new eye's very sharp but since the operation the other one's hung up its boots.'

'You've said that before, too.'

'It must be something to do with paying attention.' Sean looked at her. 'Some people have great eyesight but see very little. Others have poor hearing but hear far too much.' The girl with the harp appeared again. This time she parked it and sat at the table next to them. As she unslung her rucksack she smiled briefly in their direction. When Sean smiled back at her, she looked away but maintained the smile. He closed his bad eye and concentrated on looking at her through the good one. She was sharp, vivid. Her skin told him she was young. Taut and without blemish. There was a split in the cover of the harp she was wheeling about: a small gap. He could see marquetry – wooden pegs. Gimme a haystack and I'll find your needle. He closed his good eye and looked at her through the other, as a comparison. Sepia curtains, obscuring everything. This was the way the Impressionists saw the world. Next year he would get this eye done. And both eyes would work and he would feel young again.

The morning they did the operation a nurse had come round with a hefty black marker pen and asked him which eye. He said 'left' and she drew an arrow pointing into his left eyebrow. He knew it was an arrow because it was three deft strokes. And he was a child again playing a game, running with a piece of chalk making marks on the pavement for others to follow. It took the best part of a week for the black mark above his eyebrow to fade.

A party of young men passed through the lounge, making a lot of noise looking for the bar. They shouted that if they were going to be sick, then they needed something to be sick on. Their shouts and laughter faded as they left. Grace pulled a face of relief.

'The young ones nowadays,' she said. 'They go round with their knees outta their jeans.'

'I saw one yesterday,' said Sean. 'With things hanging from her nose like silver snot.'

Through windows to his left and right Sean could see land on both sides. Apart from 'amidships', he was no good at seagoing terms. 'Fore' and 'aft' were self-explanatory but what about 'starboard' and 'larboard'? He looked backwards, saw that they were leaving the dark clutter of cranes. This is where the *Titanic* came from. The unsinkable ship that sank. And once he'd had the thought he regretted it, because a memory of the *Princess Victoria* followed. Her going down in the Irish Sea with the loss of 130 souls to a storm in 1953. Omens all.

Grace leaned towards the girl with the harp and said, 'Batten down the hatches.'

The girl smiled.

'It mightn't be all that bad.' She stretched out her hand and rested it on the fabric covering the harp. 'Glad I didn't put this in the hold.' She sounded Irish.

'Which way is home?'

'I was raised here,' she nodded to the city. 'And I've a place where we're going. Across the water. What about yourselves?'

'We're in Scotland this long and many a day,' said Grace. 'But it's home for us now. We're neither here nor there, as the man said.'

The girl turned away and began looking for something in her rucksack. She took out her smartphone and put in ear pods.

'Only an excuse,' Sean said out of the side of his mouth, 'not to talk.'

'Make up your mind,' said his wife. 'You've just warned me about getting involved with this crowd.' She nodded to the table with the bunch of keys.

'One look at them's enough,' said Sean in a whisper.

'Then you get mad when this young one cuts me dead?'

'Maybe she's shy or something,' said Sean. 'Being wary is a two-way street.'

'Whose side are you on?' Her voice was now loud. Sean hushed her. 'It's okay,' said Grace. 'She's got ear plugs in.'

Sean looked and nodded.

Grace went on, 'Everybody's not like you. Barging in where they're not wanted.'

Sean burped a little and put his hand to his mouth.

'D'you feel queasy?'

'No. But don't look at the horizon.'

'Ever?' said Grace.

He harrumphed and turned away from her. They ceased talking. After a while she closed her eyes and allowed her chin to sink onto her chest.

The ferry emerged from the arms of the lough, and the swaying and wallowing began. When they got to the open sea, walking passengers laughed as they moved about the corridors and aisles. Little sideways staggers. Hands reaching out to steady themselves, touching chairs, handrails, pillars. Now the reason for the table rims seemed obvious.

After about half an hour the girl took out her ear pods and stood. Sean became aware of the flurry of movement. The girl glanced at him and said, 'Can you keep an eye . . . would you mind keeping an eye . . . ?'

'Are you okay?'

'Yes. I'm fine.'

'You look a bit pale.'

The girl smiled politely, then walked away as if on a tightrope, her arms out. Sean noticed a leather tag on the cover of the harp. He angled his head to read what it said. It gave a name – Lisa Boyd – followed by an address he couldn't quite make out. He was going to tell Grace but she was sound asleep. When the girl came back she was carrying a cardboard coffee cup with a lid jammed on it.

'Thank you,' she said to him. She sat and sipped her drink cautiously through the hole in the lid.

'D'you miss the place?' Sean nodded back to the Cave Hill.

The girl rolled her eyes a bit, then shook her head.

'I miss the hatred. And the bigotry. Oh and all the flegs.'

Sean laughed at her pronunciation and her bitterness. He glanced at his wife to see if she'd heard.

'Sleeping is the best thing you can do when it's like this.'

The girl nodded and smiled.

'But it's nothing like as bad as the old days,' said Sean. 'I remember bad crossings that started when you left the pier. And kept up till you docked at the other side.

Liverpool or Heysham, or wherever. There was that much sick about you'd have been far better wearing wellies.' He held up one of the plastic bags he'd plucked from the wall on the way onto the boat and said, 'Nowadays we've all the right equipment.'

'Hope we'll not need it,' said the girl.

'Do you take the harp with you everywhere?'

'I do not.'

'Well, why's it here now?'

'Because of my father.' She rolled her eyes in embarrassment. 'It's a long story.'

'It's a long journey.'

She told him about her father and how, about ten years ago, he'd had a bad fall – from scaffolding. He worked in the shipyard and somebody'd not done their job properly. Despite spending months in intensive care he was told he'd never walk again. A spinal connection had been broken.

Sean kept nodding as he listened.

'I'm sorry to hear that. That's so, so sad.'

The girl smiled as a sort of acceptance.

'And that's why you have a harp with you?' he said, with his eyebrow raised.

The girl laughed at herself. 'No, no. I'm always rambling on. Sorry.' She told him that her father liked classical music and opera. He had heard Pavarotti sing – when he was a complete unknown – in the Opera House in Belfast and had tipped him for stardom. Also he'd go to concerts and sometimes, even though she was small, he'd take her with him. He always maintained that music was a way of thinking without words. People at work thought he was odd. Later, when she showed an aptitude for it, he encouraged her to do music at school. Then a degree, then a Masters at the Royal Conservatoire in Glasgow – although at that time it was called the RSAMD. Seeing his blank look, she spelled out the Royal Scottish Academy of Music and Drama. 'The only word they left unchanged was Royal. The Scots like to bow and scrape a bit. The Royal this and the Royal that.' But her father couldn't come to her graduation because it was after his accident and – well, it was very hard for him to get about, never mind getting on and off boats.

'So when I visit him I take this,' she reached out and touched the cover of the harp. 'He wants to hear me play. To keep up with any progress.'

'That's very generous of you.'

'Sure I was coming over, anyway. To visit him.'

'Is he on his own?'

'Sadly,' she said.

'How does he manage?'

'A team come in – get him up, attend to his needs. A different crowd puts him to bed at night. He pays a woman, part housekeeper, part companion – during the day – from the compensation he got.'

'Sounds a hard road.'

'When he says listening to me playing makes him forget his condition for a while – how could I not? It's a brute to transport. Such an embarrassment. There's even jokes about it.' She mimicked a posh voice, '"*I just happen to have brought my harp.*" Everybody looks at you. But I do it for him.' She reached out and patted her instrument. 'I'd normally bring the clarsach, but this was an important birthday for him. So bigger guns were required.'

Sean looked at her face and she lowered her head. Her hair was back in a ponytail. He said, 'You're a bit of an angel.' She nodded, slightly amused. 'But are you any good at it?'

'Being an angel? Or playing the harp?'

'I thought they were the same thing.'

'Oh – I'm good enough for a man in a wheelchair.' She sipped her drink and looked up at Sean. 'So far he's been very pleased with me.'

'Aye, he must be proud.'

'It's not a word he'd ever use. One of the Seven Deadly Sins. "Pleased" is more his style.'

'Sounds good – your father. And where do you play?'

'Wherever I can get work. In the BBC orchestra mostly. And I do some teaching.'

'What's the BBC thing?'

'The Scottish Symphony Orchestra.'

'Oh, that is good,' he said. 'Maybe I better wake my wife. Save you having to say all this again. I'm beginning to forget things.'

He nudged Grace and told her in no uncertain terms who she was sitting beside. Grace sat up straight, put her hair behind her ears and blinked.

'Goodness gracious me.'

'We'll have to go to a concert the next time you play,' said Sean. 'We'll cheer you on from the sidelines.'

'Forgive me, but I'm not so keen on concerts,' said Grace. 'I never know when to clap.'

'Nothing worse,' said Sean, laughing, 'than premature clapping.'

'My father says,' the girl was laughing as she spoke, 'that you can clap when the musical argument has finally been resolved.'

'Aye, right.'

'Was I asleep for long?' said Grace. She looked down at her watch.

The girl nodded at Sean.

'He says he's beginning to forget things.'

'He doesn't have all that much to remember,' said Grace.

'What kind of music do you like?' asked the girl.

'Anything,' said Sean. 'Just so long as there's no whistling in it.'

They were now in mid-channel and the movement of the boat changed. Sean sensed the nose lifting, heard the thump of the prow as it re-entered the water. The Quiet Lounge was full of creaking noises. Grace leaned over and whispered to Sean. He nodded.

'I'd better get my drops,' he said. He stood to excuse himself. 'Tell Grace your sad story when I'm away.'

'Which one?' she smiled.

'About your dad.'

Then Sean wobbled along the runner of carpet towards the information desk.

'We're plagued with these eye-drops since his operation,' said Grace. 'One of the wee bottles has to be kept in the fridge. That's where he's away now.'

The girl made sympathetic noises.

'Another thing,' said Grace. 'He was told not to wash his hair in the shower, not to get water in his eyes for any length of time. But to do it like in an old-fashioned hairdresser's. With his head back in a wash-handbasin. So who do you think had to do it this morning before we left?'

'You?'

Grace nodded. 'I was a hairdresser before we were married. In the days of the permanent wave.'

'A bit like today,' said the girl, nodding towards the weather.

'You've never heard of "a permanent wave"? Daughter dear, you must be very young.' The girl smiled in response. 'Of course nowadays almost everybody looks young to us. But Sean said you'd a story to tell?'

And she told Grace the reason she had her harp with her.

Sean came back with a paper cup containing his dropper bottles.

'I didn't fancy doing it in front of everybody at the desk,' he said. 'Like some sort of a performance.'

'Have you washed your hands?'

'Yes,' he said. He set down his paper cup and, like a child, showed her both his gleaming hands. 'There was a brave few in the toilets throwing up, by the sound of it.' He turned to the harpist. 'If you'll excuse me saying so.'

Grace steadied the paper cup and Sean took out the first of his eye-dropper bottles. He adopted his stance – legs wide apart, wrists clear of his sleeves, his head back, chin up.

'A drop in the ocean,' he said.

'You're just not funny any more,' Grace said. The first one missed – the second hit the target. Sean turned to his wife, his face running with liquid.

'If it gets as far as your mouth, it tastes vile.' He wiped his cheek with his handkerchief. 'The boat's swaying so much I missed.' Then the same palaver with the second bottle. The wrists, the legs, the head, his eye staring at the wobbling drop hanging from the nozzle. 'I can never get used to the splash – especially when it's so cold.'

This time the eye brimmed over. He sat down and put his head back so that the drops would be effective for longer. To balance himself he stretched out his feet to rest on his wife's chair. Grace went on talking to the girl.

'Do you have to grow your nails?'

'No.'

'People playing the guitar sometimes do.'

'We play with our fingerpads,' said the girl. 'Except for the pinkie.'

'You don't use your wee finger?'

'Naw. It's redundant.' There was a long pause. 'Do you mind me asking – what are the drops for?'

Sean interrupted. And, talking to the ceiling, he told the story of his cataracts. How, with age, he'd noticed everything had reduced in sharpness. Lettering was indistinct. He could see a bus coming but not know its number. The final straw was when he was told he was not legal to drive. So they operated on his eye and put a new lens in. The girl shuddered loudly.

'When did all this happen?'

'Two weeks ago. They'll do the other eye in a month or two.'

'I hate anything to do with eyes,' said the girl, tightening her mouth. 'It gives me the squeams.'

'Don't talk,' said Grace. 'I'm beginning to feel a bit queasy myself.'

'We're more than halfway,' said Sean. 'It's not going to get any worse.'

A lot of people had created room for themselves and lain down and closed their eyes. Some made room on the floor. Grace leaned forward to the girl.

'What's your name?'

'Lisa.'

Sean raised his head but did not sit up.

'And your father?'

'He's John.'

'Aye, I saw your name on the tag on your harp,' said Sean.

'Your eyesight can't be all that bad,' said Lisa.

There was silence. The thump of the ship's prow into the waves had become less frequent and the wind seemed to be dropping. The Quiet Lounge was quiet for the first time. Grace smiled and told her their names.

'And your father worked in the Yard?'

'It's not what you think. We're the same as yourselves.'

She told them of her family tree, of some ancestor called Boyd who came from England and fell for a girl called Gallagher. She made a Catholic of him. And in the shipyard he lived in fear his secret would be discovered and 'the red-hot rivets would rain down on him' from the other side.

'That was the way he put it,' said Lisa.

'It's a strange world,' said Grace. They all smiled and looked about them. 'D'you play any Irish music?'

'Yes, I do. Jigs and reels and what-have-you. My father's very fond of it. And him unable to tap his feet. O'Carolan is his favourite.'

'Oh, he's the boy,' said Sean, still lying down. 'He was as blind as a bat. Smallpox at the age of eighteen. They say he composed on horseback. Riding round Ireland.'

Grace looked down at him.

'How could he ride around Ireland if he was blind?' she said.

'He was led. By a man. Who knew the way.'

'And how have you become such an expert on this subject?'

'Books. In work.'

Grace rolled her eyes and turned away from him to the girl.

'Would you play for us?' she said.

The girl laughed. She indicated with her hand all the people sitting in the lounge.

'They may not want to listen,' she said. 'And it's the Quiet Lounge.'

'That would embarrass you then?' said Grace.

'Yes and no. It'd feel a bit odd. If anyone objected . . . '

'Leave the girl alone,' said Sean.

Lisa tried to change the subject. 'You were a hairdresser,' she said. She turned to Sean, 'And what about you?'

'I was a librarian. Used to blow the dust off the top of the books.' He stood and half crouched to see out the window. It was difficult – spume adhered to the glass and made what was beyond indistinct. But at least the colour now had some green and brown in it.

'Land ho!' He pointed to the window. 'That's the way I used to see.'

'Or not see,' said Grace.

Sean leaned forward, his face almost against the glass. Three seabirds were flying alongside. White birds with black wingtips. 'Would you look at them?' he said. There was something about them – the way they were flying in a close triangular formation, their determined rowing into the wind, keeping pace with the ferry. Maybe sheltering in the lee of the boat.

Lisa raised herself to see what he was talking about.

'Gannets,' she said.

'Glad to see them. How wonderful.'

'We seem to be through the worst of it,' Lisa said. 'It's calming down a bit. We'll be in in no time.'

'Just enough time for you to play for us,' said Grace. 'Please.'

Lisa pulled a face.

'Please?' The girl maintained the look of reluctance. 'Sure don't you play in public at every turn-round.' Grace began to pretend to applaud, clapping her hands silently. 'Please, please, please?'

'Go easy,' said Sean. 'She might be shy. Mightn't want to.'

Lisa rolled her eyes and smiled at the same time.

'It's not that,' she said.

'Just for me,' Grace was pretending to wheedle.

'Only if these people don't mind.' Lisa stood.

'Good for you,' said Grace, patting her shoulder. Lisa consulted the nearest tables, asking if they minded her playing. Pointing to the harp. Of course they were all for it. She came back to her own table and began to take the cover off.

'My father says it looks like a giant oven glove.'

Sean smiled and nodded.

'So it does,' he said. 'Or a wonky heart.' He began to clear an area to give her enough room.

Lisa removed the cover, and Grace showed she was impressed. It was so far removed from the everyday, this thing, made of various shades of wood standing above head height, bristling with tuning pegs. Pale strings cross-hatched the wood frame, some of different colours, red, blue, green.

'Oh my God,' said Grace. 'What a lovely thing.'

Everyone in the Quiet Lounge was now aware of what was going on and if they were lying down, they were nudged to get up. And if they stood up, they were nudged to one side. Some swayed to and fro on their seats to get a better view. The girl in the wheelchair made a U-turn and faced the front. The man with the elderly family elbowed the woman beside him and she followed the direction of his look, saw the harp and raised her eyebrows in delight. The silvered metal of the tuning pegs reflected the lights.

Lisa tugged down her jumper and sat in close to the instrument. Her feet in black lace-up boots found the range of the pedals. She cleared her throat and leaned towards Sean.

'I'm not nervous about playing,' she said quietly. 'But talking gives me the heebie-jeebies. I'll play all night – just so long as I don't have to say anything.'

'Be not afeard,' said Sean and laughed. He gave a hand flourish, 'the isle is full of noises, sounds and sweet airs

231

that give delight and hurt not.' Lisa's brow wrinkled up at the change in his tone. '*The Tempest*,' he said. Then, taking what Lisa had said as a hint, he got to his feet and banged the table with the heel of a bottle. 'A bit of shush, please. If you don't mind.' People looked up and the place quietened. 'Conditions are rough, and my wife has been pestering this woman to play her harp – to calm us all down – to lift us above the waters – and she has finally and, somewhat reluctantly, agreed.'

Lisa finished her tuning checks and, when she was satisfied, began to play.

And as she played the room became hushed and truly quiet – listening-quiet. People changed their seats so that they no longer had their backs to the harpist. While he'd been speaking, someone took Sean's seat and he had to remain standing. The rolling movement of Lisa's hands, each note following hard upon the other, like the waves, tumbling one over the other, cascading. Like the rhythm of the sea itself. Sean watched the girl's face. Watched the whirl of her hands. This was not somebody who was trying to remember the piece – she was a true musician. Convincing listeners that it could not be played any other way – playing it afresh – as if it was being made up on the spot. The girl in the wheelchair by this time had taken out her mobile and was holding it up, filming.

And as the arms of land enclosed them, the movement of the ferry steadied. It no longer lurched or swooped but eased smoothly forward, as it entered the shelter of the Scottish hills. Behind the ferry the white wake widened. The harpist moved from one musical piece to the next – or maybe it was all one piece – maybe they were different movements from the same piece. She segued from fast to slow, from sad to sweet. Then stopped. And the Quiet Lounge was loud with applause.

Grace was clapping her hands as hard as she could, smacking them together. She stopped and spoke loudly to Lisa, 'Your poor pinkies never got a look-in.'

Lisa smiled, then turned to the audience and played again. And each time she stopped, the people clapped. Grace did not care whether or not it was the wrong place to clap. She was astonished at Lisa's skill and she was enjoying herself.

At the next ending Lisa heard out the applause. She seemed shy and waved the people to silence. 'I hope you don't mind but I was asked to play as a favour by my friends here. And I couldn't refuse them.' Her voice was a little tremulous as she named the composers of the pieces she had just played. 'I see we're nearly there. So I'd like to end with something Irish . . . Emigration was one of the saddest things ever to have happened in Ireland – both north and south. The people who left because of the famine, years ago, didn't have much to carry. Music is light luggage. But as the saying goes, "songs make an easy bundle". Here's one of them.'

New people were coming to the Quiet Lounge and standing in the doorways. They whispered to one another, trying to find out what was happening. Who was the musician? What was the occasion? Did they have to pay?

From his standing position Sean could see ahead and sideways. Everything through his good eye was so sharp. Colours so much brighter. The light flashed from the water. And he noticed the three gannets as they sailed into view again. They'd kept abreast now for about fifteen minutes, moving up to deck level, now dropping to skim the sea. Sometimes beating their wings, sometimes gliding. But always keeping their formation. Why were they heading towards land with such determination? Why did they choose such a day to make their crossing? Their flying seemed to have such urgency and grace, keeping time with the music, which told of convoys – parties of mourning the night before departure from home – living wakes for those who would never be seen again, be they bound for the Antipodes or the Americas. The audience clapped so much Lisa felt obliged to play an encore.

'Something by O'Carolan,' shouted Sean.

She nodded and began a rousing march. People tapped their feet, nodded their heads in time to the music. Sean became aware again of this girl's kindness to her father and imagined him in his wheelchair listening, allowing these very notes to briefly dissolve away his pain. And on top of this he imagined O'Carolan in his cave of permanent darkness, conceiving the notes. How could he know that, centuries later, it would move a man and his wife, travelling through rough seas between Ireland and their home. But then, if he was an artist, how could he *not* know?

BLACKTHORNS

County Derry 1942

The man walked the road with his two little girls. They came to a small bridge where there was a gap in the hedge that would allow them to go down to the burn. Some branches were in the way and the man held them to one side with his arm so the girls could go through. When the innermost part of the hedge was revealed, he had a look to see if there were any likely sticks. He let the branches spring back again and, in doing so, one scratched the back of his hand.

When he was out walking with his daughters he liked to show them things. If he found an empty bird's nest he would lift them up to peep into it. He would tell them it was now 'their' nest. But they must never touch it because the bird would then forsake it. Every time they passed this spot, they would remember. And they could have nests all over the woods. As well as holes where badgers lived. And wet places for frogspawn. And where the biggest blackberries were in autumn.

They went down to the stream. It was shallow and the fast water flowed noisily over the stones. In some places it fanned white over larger rocks. The sound the burn made was continual.

'Can we build a dam?' asked the elder girl. Their father nodded. He was pleased because it was he who had taught them to do this in the first place. But he started them off by lifting some large stones and splashing them into place.

'Careful, Anne.' Their father declared that the water was too cold at this time of year for them to go barefoot. The girls wore grey socks and strappy shoes. They balanced on dry stones, crouched on flat ones, dug downwards with their fingers into the silt and mud and gravel. They did not allow their hands to remain in the water for long, but took them out and shook life back into them. 'Anne, keep an eye on Clare. Don't let her get too cold. And don't ruin your shoes or your mother'll kill me.'

He left them to it and wandered upstream. He looked at where the branch had scratched him and licked away the blood. At this time of year the wood was devoid of any flowers. He headed up the slope into the trees. What he loved was the quiet, with only the occasional bird call. And the now-distant sounds and squeals of his two daughters as they played. It was late afternoon and the light was beginning to disappear. He loved the way the trees grew straight upwards, regardless of the tilt of the land. As if they took their orders from the centre of the earth and not from the slant of the forest floor. They had shed most of their leaves and the sky was visible when he looked up through the canopy. He was now approaching the big house and could just see some of the turrets and chimneypots. As the light faded, everything became very sharp against the sky.

There was something unusual going on. He could hear noises he did not associate with the big house. Many voices, laughter, the sound of heavy engines. Where the path turned, it afforded him a view of the rear of the big house and its yards and stables. The area was full of sol-diers criss-crossing the muddied yard. Carrying stuff, emptying lorries. There was boogie-woogie music coming from somewhere. A gramophone? Or was it a real piano from the big house? The sound was drowned by a soldier revving the engine of his jeep. His wheels were just spinning in the mud, and his vehicle was drifting slowly from side to side. From this distance there was something odd about the scene, which he couldn't make out. He went off the path to get a closer look, his feet ploughing through undergrowth and nettles. He was brought up short by an old wire fence. When he looked up again he realised that all the uniformed men were black-skinned – every last one of them. He had never seen such a thing before. Photographs, yes, but living people in front of his eyes? Then he realised that these must be the first American Negro troops to arrive. He watched and mar-velled for a while, then called the girls to show them.

Almost every test the doctor performed gave him cause for concern. Temperature, blood pressure, the wound itself. He tried not to let it show on his face. The man's wife stood at the other side of the bed watching, willing things to have a remedy. The man was lying on his back with his eyes closed. He wore a grey semmit and his hands were cold and clammy to the touch. His black stubble seemed to weigh on his face. It was difficult to tell if he was conscious or not. The ground-floor bedroom was small and airless and through the painted-shut window the doctor could see into the street. The front door slammed and a girl appeared outside, carrying a white-enamelled pail. By the way she carried it, it was empty. She was no more than twelve. She wore a flowered frock, up-and-down at the hem, and a grey cardigan for warmth. The child had no notion of what was going on with her father because she danced the last few steps to the pump. From such a distance the doctor could hear the dry squeak when the girl worked the pump handle and, more faintly, the water gushing into the pail.

He took up the man's wrist from the coverlet again and found the pulse point. He checked it against his pocket watch. There was a small crucifix on the wall and, above the bed, a picture marked with a caption, *Mother of Perpetual Succour*. These images were in nearly all Roman Catholic houses. The most popular one – although absent here – was of the Lord displaying his red heart. The breathing of the man in the bed could be heard at the end of each quick exhalation. Three nails had been driven into the back of the bedroom door. On the central nail hung a navy-blue overall or housecoat in the vague shape of the human being who had previously worn it. The other two nails were vacant. When he let go of the man's wrist, it flopped down. By now the girl was on her way back to the house with her bucket, her arm straight out from her shoulder for balance. Her breath was visible on the winter air. He indicated to the man's wife that he had finished his examination and they both turned to leave the room.

In the kitchen the doctor faced the woman. He was tall and the woman had to look up at him. He could see in her eyes that she was ignorant of the seriousness of her husband's condition. So he found it difficult to get the words together. The front door opened and the girl came in with the half-filled pail of water. It was all she could manage to carry. She set the white bucket with its turquoise water under the table and gathered herself into an old armchair beside the hearth. The doctor glanced at the child and lowered his voice.

'I'm afraid, Mrs Conway, that . . . ' He looked again at the girl in the armchair.

Her mother said, 'Why don't you go outside and play with your sisters?'

The child did as she was told. The doctor smiled at her as she passed him. Her hair was blonde and tangled. The latch on the front door clicked shut.

'Mrs Conway, your husband is a very sick man,' he said. The mother's chin moved repeatedly and she found it very difficult to know where to begin. 'Can you tell me again what happened? Is there anything else I should know?'

'At the start of the week he was out walking the roads as usual,' the woman said. She pressed her index finger to her temple as if it would help her recall. 'He had two of the children with him and he got a bit of a scratch. Said he was looking for blackthorn sticks out of a hedge beyond Coyle's Bridge. It's something Peter does – to try and make a few shillings.' The doctor listened carefully, his head inclined. 'He thought nothing of it. But the other night he showed me the redness and the swelling. The next day he took to his bed with the shivers – and that's not like him – so I sent for the doctor.' She must have thought it sounded unmannerly, 'For you, Dr Irvine.'

'His bloodstream is poisoned. I've seen this condition before.' He shook his head. Then he noticed the picture on the kitchen wall of Jesus displaying his heart. This was bad enough, but even worse was the glow of a filament of a red lamp in front of it. He sidestepped the woman so that his back was to the picture. 'I cannot emphasise too much the seriousness of his condition. He may not survive.' The woman's eyes widened in disbelief and then she hid her face from him with both hands.

'He's a fit man,' she said into her cupped hands. 'Aw, Peter dear.' She seemed ashamed to be upset in front of the doctor.

'We'll do our best,' said Dr Irvine. 'We'll do our very best for him.'

Outside on the street the doctor took a deep breath, tried to clear the muffled feeling of the small house from his lungs. He slipped the coins the woman had paid him into his trouser pocket – aware that it was, for such a household, a substantial sum. Probably they'd pawned something or borrowed from somebody better off than themselves. He knew that Peter Conway had no work to speak of – other than what he earned from odd jobs. He had never given him any work himself, but he had seen him digging and clipping hedges and cutting grass about the town. Dr Irvine kept those kind of jobs for the not-so-well-off on his own side of the house. If Conway died, his whole family would have to sit on an egg less.

Rain, not enough to darken the ground, had started. It was his last house call of the day, hardly worth driving the car home. In the square, soldiers were drilling. American infantrymen. Shouted commands mixed with the sound of crows cawing behind the church above the trees. Unlike the British, they marched three abreast instead of four. He rolled down the window and listened to the pulse of their boots as they wheeled and turned. They were good, unlike their reputation. The British troops, who had been there before them, mocked them – accusing them of slovenly saluting, of a casual approach to uniform. But that was only to be expected. All tradesmen did it – criticised their rivals. A joiner he'd hired to install their kitchen complained, 'Whoever did this job the first time never heard of measuring.'

And from where he sat, the engine idling, he could see an American face he actually knew. The US Army had arrived earlier in the week, hard on the heels of the departure of the Royal Berkshires, and Dr Irvine had been invited to the welcoming reception.

'You bring bright horizons,' he said to every Yank he spoke to. 'Your intervention is timely and will be decisive.' He was conscious of using cut-glass language and diction and he did not want to embarrass the American visitors by colloquialisms. He had been introduced to the doctor in charge, Major Bradley Zelinski. And there he was, as large as life, on the steps of the hotel in the town square, taking the salute. At the reception he and the Major had had a long chat. Dr Irvine was impressed and had invited him to his house that evening.

He did not want to interrupt the manoeuvres, so he drove the back road home. Once inside the house, the first thing he did was to phone the hospital to see if they could render him any assistance with his case of septicaemia. But it was late in the day and there was a war on. Perhaps tomorrow. Was that the very best he could do? Deep down, he knew that tomorrow would be too late. He shrugged even though there was no one in the room.

For some time the doctor's wife, Myrtle, had been excited at the prospect of 'a villageful of Cary Grants', but knowing she was to welcome one of them into her house so soon was hardly believable. The morning after the reception she'd sent their housemaid, Winnie, in search of ingredients. Winnie put pressure on the butcher and, by the afternoon, he came up with a plump chicken for Dr Irvine. The greengrocer handed over a leathery but fresh pamphrey. And the potatoes were the best available. So that in no time at all everyone in the town knew the Irvines were having an American visitor. What Winnie could not buy, Myrtle borrowed from friends. It was an occasion important enough to use her wedding china, Royal Doulton, which she kept in the glass china cabinet. Winnie had been instructed to wash and dry each item, just in case.

All afternoon during surgery hours the doctor had heard the two women scurrying about the house. Once, between patients, he went to see what all the fuss was about. Myrtle confessed she thought roast chicken and pamphrey sounded a bit odd.

'There's a war on,' said the doctor.

'I think he might know that.'

Myrtle made her husband say the Major's name aloud so that she could pronounce and practise it.

In the hallway when he arrived that evening in full uniform, Dr Irvine introduced him to his wife.

'This is Major Bradley Zelinski.'

'Call me Brad,' he said and shook hands firmly with Myrtle. The sound of the jeep, which had left him at the door, roared off into the night. Winnie, in her white freshly starched apron, took his coat and set his peaked cap on the polished hall table. Myrtle thought the Major had a wonderful smile. His uniform was a jacket of dark chocolate-brown, beige trousers with stone-coloured shirt and tie. He brought gifts of Chesterfield cigarettes and Jack Daniel's bourbon and looked like he had stepped straight out of Hollywood.

When they sat down to table, Dr Irvine and his wife bowed their heads and said grace. The Major looked down at his place setting. When Winnie brought in the food the Major ate the American way, cutting up with his knife, then spearing and scooping with his fork. He talked slowly and well. Mostly about FDR. And when he saw the puzzlement on their faces at the first mention of the initials he added, 'Roosevelt'. He then went on to speak of Churchill and asked them what they thought of him. The Irvines were hesitant but eventually said he was no friend to Ulster – a devious man, if ever there was one.

'Ever know a politician who was *not* devious?' Brad said.

'I like the way you *drawl*,' said Myrtle and they all laughed at her forwardness. They could tell Brad was paying close attention to the way *they* spoke because he would ask Myrtle to repeat some things. But she charged on at the same speed and took no account of Brad's unfamiliarity with local Irish words or constructions or expressions. As for Brad, he tried to put his hostess at her ease by frequently telling her he was having a swell time. His face was suntanned and leathery, which made his teeth seem whiter. Myrtle could hardly take her eyes off him all night.

After the food, which the Major praised extravagantly, especially the gravy, he offered around his cigarettes. The Irvines didn't smoke very much, but they knew how to do it.

'I'm considered a bit eccentric,' said Dr Irvine. 'I remain to be convinced it's harmless.' For the evening Myrtle declared herself 'a social smoker' and Brad got up from his place to light her cigarette. She detailed Winnie to bring in an ashtray. It took some time before the maid found one. It was a freebie Dr Irvine had got at a medical conference, advertising Player's Navy Cut. At each corner there was a small indentation to rest your cigarette. Myrtle kept tapping hers, sometimes sharpening the ash against the rim.

When she asked him where he was from, Brad said the Midwest. Iowa. His mother was Irish – thus the perpetuation of the family name Bradley – and his father Polish. He was brought up on farming territory. He knew about going to bed early and the brutal times of rising. Of working all the daylight hours God sent. Of horizons that were uninterrupted, and roads that were ruler-straight because there was little reason for them to become bends. Of temperatures you would not believe – summers hot enough to fry eggs on the tarmac, winters cold enough to freeze your brains when you inhaled.

Dr Irvine apologised, said that they could not make coffee well enough to please an American but they were good at tea, adding, 'We have insufficient equipment.'

'Equipment?'

'A percolator. I asked every shop in the town but nobody would own up to one. We have, however, all the accommodation for making excellent tea.' The Major didn't seem to like the idea of tea, but thought he'd like a glass of the in-store bourbon that he'd brought.

The Irvines were abstemious people who went to church every Sunday. Their eyes kept meeting, almost as a warning – 'Watch your step,' they seemed to say to each other. Dr Irvine took the Jack Daniel's from the sideboard and, after a moment's hesitation, handed it to the Major to open. Myrtle took out a glass from the china cabinet and set it on the table. She looked up at her husband. He sheepishly nodded yes. She set another glass on the table. Brad opened the bottle and poured two glasses. They all listened to the quiet popping the American whisky made in the neck of the bottle as it came out.

'Are you sure you'll not join us?' said the Major to Myrtle. She shook her head shyly.

'We're not big ones for the booze,' she said.

'Here's to the man himself,' said Brad, making a toast. 'To Jack Daniel.'

He drank off his glass.

'And to FDR for coming to help,' said Dr Irvine.

He sipped his drink slowly, as if it was scalding. He reached out, turned the bottle and read the label.

'Lynchburg, Tennessee. Not a great name for a town in the Deep South.'

The Major looked at him. One of his eyebrows went up.

'It's not what you think,' said Brad. 'Rumour has it – the town was started up by a fellow countryman of yours, an Irishman called Lynch.'

Dr Irvine laughed. There was a pause, then he said, 'I saw some soldiers, earlier this afternoon – a column of them driving into the big-house gates. They were . . . '

Brad nodded.

'That'll be our coloured boys. Odd-job specialists, not fit for combat. Looking after latrines and the like. Stay well away, if you know what's good for you.'

'Oh, don't talk,' said Myrtle. 'Everywhere you go there's somebody who'll let the side down.'

Brad looked at his plate and smiled.

'You might laugh, but I knew a Major-General – good friend of mine, who shall be nameless – and he said if he had to choose between having five thousand white soldiers or two hundred and fifty thousand coloured boys . . . ' he looked at the Irvines, challenging them to guess. Dr Irvine and Myrtle hesitated. 'Said he'd go for the whites every time.'

'And where are you based?' asked Myrtle.

'The camp out at Lismoyne.'

'So it's a segregated army?'

'We wanna win the war.'

'*A house divided against itself*,' said Dr Irvine. 'Mark, chapter three, verse twenny-five.'

'Listen to *you*,' said Myrtle, 'picking up an accent already.'

'You have no idea. Can you imagine those black boys managing the amount of medical supplies I have out there. Whole operating theatres plus equipment and backup, ready to move at a moment's notice. Ready to mop up the war.'

'We have a thing here called the Black Preceptory,' said Dr Irvine, smiling. He put his elbows on the table and leaned closer to the American. 'It's a religious thing and some people refer to them as "black men".'

'And are they?'

'No.' Dr Irvine laughed. 'Have you heard of the Orange Order?'

Brad nodded.

'Yes. Don't tell me they're orange.' He waited for a laugh but none was forthcoming. 'I'm kidding,' he said. 'They briefed us a little about it before we came over.'

'Well, I'm a member of the Black Preceptory. A black man, if you like.' They all seemed amused. 'You progress through the Orange Order to the heights of – the black men are supposed to be a bit more respectable. Being a doctor helps. The Imperial Grand Black Chapter of the British Commonwealth, to give it the full title.'

'And what do you do?'

'They parade to church in full regalia,' said Myrtle.

Brad smiled at her.

'And do you set fire to crosses?'

Dr Irvine's face remained solemn.

'No, we don't.'

Brad turned to Myrtle.

'And the women?'

'It's a Protestant *fraternal* society,' said Dr Irvine. 'There are no women.'

'We're sidelined,' said Myrtle, 'except when it comes to work.'

Brad picked up the bottle and tilted it towards his host's glass. Dr Irvine put his finger and thumb almost together to indicate how little he required. Brad seemed to ignore the gesture. Dr Irvine shook his head because, he said, in a town this size he was always on duty. Nevertheless he sipped what had been poured and smiled at the Major. Winnie came in and began to clear the rest of the table. The two men became more and more deeply absorbed in a conversation about the nature of small-town medicine. So much so that Myrtle excused herself, closed the kitchen door and began to help Winnie with the dishes, so as the maid could get home early.

Dr Irvine said that he felt he had a vocation to look after all the people of the town, whatever their religious persuasion. It was drudgery, but it was necessary drudgery. It was work of high seriousness – daily he dealt with matters of life and death. And Brad nodded, inhaling his cigarette. Dr Irvine said that in war or peacetime there was no better thing they could be doing. Bringing children into the world, reducing their neighbour's ration of pain, smoothing the exit of the old. The rewards were not financial. Brad nodded vigorously. He joked that his bank, instead of sending him columns of figures, should send him a note to say, 'You have enough.'

'That's all we need,' he said.

Dr Irvine said that he was frequently paid in plucked chickens, new potatoes and bunches of rhubarb.

Brad poured himself another glass but Dr Irvine refused absolutely, saying it was 'a very strong brew for someone who is practically teetotal'.

But there is deep sadness in the everyday, too, said Dr Irvine. He told of his visit to the poor family that afternoon and how it had affected him. The man had septicaemia. He had a wife and four young daughters. The man might even have died – as they were speaking. He was only in his early forties.

Brad shook his head in sympathy. Myrtle must have overheard from the kitchen because she came into the room and said, 'Who are we talking about?'

'I don't think you'd know them,' said Dr Irvine. 'The Conways. Live down by the burn near the school. They've four girls, wouldn't you know.'

'Roman Catholics,' said Myrtle, to keep Brad informed. 'I've seen them about.'

Brad looked from one to the other. Myrtle returned to the kitchen.

'I might have something . . . out at the camp,' said Brad.

'Like what?'

'Antibacterial juice. It's new. Can be very effective.'

'So what is it?'

Brad told him the trade name and the success rate of the trials in America.

'The Scotchman and his Petri dish discovered it ages ago. Fleming. But we were the only ones who could mass-produce the stuff.'

'Like Henry Ford?'

'Henry was some man. Put America on its feet.'

'I would have thought the opposite. Because of Henry Ford, nobody walks any more.'

'*Financially* on its feet.' Brad laughed and slapped the table. 'Some man, Henry. Very fond of employing the coloureds.' He shook his head and chuckled. 'But he's not fond of the Jew-boys. So they say.'

'Not a big problem here.'

Brad went on to outline the method of deep-tank fermentation that was necessary to mass-produce the anti-bacterial juice. Dr Irvine listened and nodded.

'I know what you're talking about. I'm sure I've read about this in *The Lancet*.'

'I can let you have some.'

'It's probably too late.'

'In the evening?'

'No. I mean he's probably passed away.'

'We can get it right now – if you drive me out to the camp.'

Dr Irvine considered this. He looked towards the kitchen door, then glanced at his pocket watch.

'Are you sure?'

'It's late, but . . . '

'The sooner, the better,' said Dr Irvine, easing himself to his feet. Brad drank off his glass and stood.

'I hate waste,' he said, staring down at Dr Irvine's half-emptied glass. 'Down in one.'

Dr Irvine hesitated, then finished his drink in two long sips. He opened the kitchen door and spoke to his wife to explain where they were going.

'Will you be back?'

'I doubt it.'

She gave him a look, then flung the dishcloth into the sink.

They drove out the Lismoyne Road. Dr Irvine sat high in his seat trying to see ahead as best he could with his attenuated headlights. He was also a little nervous about the amount of alcohol he had just consumed.

'What's the car?' said Brad.

'Austin Ten.' There was a long pause. Dr Irvine added, 'I'm very fond of it.'

'It's a first for me. Are you getting enough fuel?'

'I'm probably the only man in the town who is.'

On one bend the car began to drift and Dr Irvine steered into the skid to regain control.

'I didn't realise it was so slippy,' he said. 'Must be black ice.'

'Slick,' said Brad. 'That's the word we use. Slick.'

Dr Irvine took his foot off the accelerator. He'd been told that the slowest speed in the highest gear gave the most traction.

When they arrived at the camp Brad talked them through security, then directed Dr Irvine along a cement road lined with Nissen huts to a red-brick building. A field had become a street in a matter of weeks. Dr Irvine parked. The Major invited him to come in and have a look around.

'I think the sooner we get to the patient, the more chance we have,' said Dr Irvine.

Brad got out of the car and the door slammed. Dr Irvine kept the engine running.

He was frightened of the effect of the bourbon. Brad seemed to be immune to it. Uniformed white soldiers moved about the place, talking loudly, laughing.

He rested his forehead on the steering wheel. Never again. After a while Brad came back with a bagful of kit. Dr Irvine leaned across the front seat and let him in.

'On, James, and don't spare the horses,' said Brad in a mock, not-very-good English accent. Dr Irvine drove – slow as a learner. He concentrated on the road and the possibility of ice, so much so that he understood little of what Brad said about Pfizer's production of large quantities of pharmaceutical-grade antibacterial juice.

The place was dark and Dr Irvine felt around for a door knocker. He gave up and hammered on the door with his fist. There were reverberations as if the door was not a good fit. A sound of movement from inside and Mrs Conway opened the latch. She was dressed in a navy shower-of-hail overall and looked up, startled, at the two men.

'Sorry to disturb you at this time,' said Dr Irvine. 'But there is another treatment we'd like to try with your husband.'

The woman looked over her shoulder into the house and dropped her voice.

'Oh, we can't afford . . . '

'Never mind about that. It's a kind of research for us. My colleague is American. Dr Bradley Zelinski. For a second opinion.'

'Two doctors? How could I pay two doctors?'

Brad reached out and shook hands with the woman.

'How is he at the moment?'

'Very poorly,' she said. 'He was anointed earlier.'

Even in the dim light Dr Irvine could see her distress.

'Has the priest gone?'

'Yes – he left about half an hour ago.'

Dr Irvine and Brad had to stoop a little going through the front door. The kitchen was warm and a kettle was sizzling on the range. Two of the elder girls were still up, including the one with the tangled blonde hair Dr Irvine had seen earlier.

Both the doctors greeted the girls in subdued voices. The girls nodded but did not say anything. Then there was a noise from the far end of the room and two small heads appeared. The woman of the house told them in an angry whisper to go back to bed, and then led the way into the sick man's bedroom. She switched on the single bulb. Dr Irvine could smell the candle wax in the air after the anointing ceremony. He was unsure of the name for it or any of the other mumbo-jumbo that went on. The extinguished candle with its black wick stood on a stool.

Brad went to the bed and tried to assess the situation. He got no response from the man. Dr Irvine looked at the woman and moved his eyes towards the bedroom door. She nodded and left them alone.

'The anointing means they think he's going to die,' said Dr Irvine.

'I know. I'm Polish.'

Dr Irvine watched Brad open his medical pack and produce a black box. Everything was marked as property of the US Government. In the box was a glass syringe. He took a tablet from a small jar of tablets and added one into the barrel of the syringe, then drew up a certain amount of solution from a different container. The back of his chocolate jacket looked black as he stooped in the dim light to inspect the man's arm on the coverlet.

'Do you want me to . . . ' said Dr Irvine.

'No, I'm fine,' said Brad. He waited for the tablet to dissolve and turned to Dr Irvine, rolling his eyes a little in impatience. He gave the syringe a shake to assist the dissolving. Then, when he felt the process was complete, he pointed the needle to the ceiling and squeezed out a little fountain towards the light bulb. He injected the whole syringe.

The two doctors came back the next morning. Mrs Conway remained in the kitchen with her girls. The patient lay in the bed, his eyes open. His breathing was too fast and shallow. Dr Irvine introduced Major Zelinski to the patient, explaining that not only was he a Major, but also a doctor.

'This is Peter Conway.'

The patient laboriously turned his head to look at the uniformed man.

'How do you feel?'

'Not so good,' said Peter.

Dr Irvine went through the same battery of tests as he'd done the night before.

'But you're still with us.'

'I am.'

All three men smiled.

It was Dr Irvine who did the second injection. When the needle went in, the man reacted by straightening his lips.

On the third visit the patient had changed his grey semmit for a white vest and was sitting up in bed, clean-shaven, with his arms folded. Mrs Conway came into the room with the two doctors. Dr Irvine noticed that the candle and the altar cloth were no longer there. A fire had been lit in the bedroom grate and it made the room seem a little more hospitable. There were kindling sticks and halved logs in the hearth.

'I think my prayers have been answered,' she said. 'He's on the mend – took tea and toast this morning. And shaved himself. One of the girls held the mirror.'

'This is truly remarkable,' said Dr Irvine. He had no need to go through his battery of tests. He could just see the improvement. But Brad was more efficient. He did his tests and found them all normal, or returning to normal. Even the site of the original scratch had lost its redness and swelling. What was taking place was healing.

'We'll have you back to work in no time,' he said.

'If only . . . ' said Mrs Conway. 'If only it was as simple as that.'

Brad gave him a final injection, just to be on the safe side. The fire made spitting and cracking noises.

When Brad had finished, Peter scratched his hair with both hands and said, 'I mind very little about the last couple of days. Clare tells me you've both been great.' His wife nodded. 'We don't have very much, but I'd like to . . . I make sticks – walking sticks. I've a selection of good ones out in the shed. They're not quite ready for action but as soon as I'm on my feet again, I'll get them round to ye.'

Both doctors smiled and nodded their thanks, not quite believing it would happen.

Outside the patient's house the two doctors stood talking.

'Hey – that's some stuff. I'm very grateful to you,' said Dr Irvine. 'I've never seen anything like it. From death's door to fighting fit, all in the space of . . . '

'About thirty-six hours.' Brad's face indicated that he too still thought it pretty amazing.

He stamped his feet.

'The cold here gets into your bones. It's so damp.'

There was a jeep parked in the driveway and the house was warm and full of the aroma of coffee. Winnie loaded up a tray and brought it into the sitting room.

'Thank you,' said Myrtle. 'It's maybe not as good as you can make it, Brad.'

Winnie raised her eyebrows but said nothing.

Brad offered Myrtle a cigarette and she became a social smoker again. He lit hers first, then his own. She'd touched his arm to guide the flame to her. She loved the clunk it made when he closed his lighter.

The two men stood looking out the window. There was sleet blowing occasionally across the garden. Against the dark tarmacadam drive it appeared as hailstones.

When Brad took the first sip of his coffee he said, 'Another tutorial on the percolator might be required.' He laughed and apologised, saying he was only joking.

'Be much simpler if you tried to like tea,' said Myrtle. 'Coffee and Ulster scones don't seem to go together.' She blew out the smoke away from the company.

*

A man and two young girls walked into the driveway.

'Who's this?' said Dr Irvine. 'So much for helping the war effort. They take your gates away and anybody can wander in.'

'I know who it is,' said Myrtle. 'Conway – who lives down near the school.'

'Our famous patient,' said Brad.

'I wonder what he wants?' said Dr Irvine.

'I don't want them in here,' said Myrtle. 'That's for sure.'

Peter Conway looked up and saw the group standing in the bay window. He gave directions to his girls, who were each carrying a stick. Then he took the sticks from them and looked up at his audience. He pretended to be stooped over and put his weight on both sticks, pretended to be crippled even. He went on with this charade for some time, looking up and grinning.

'Is he trying to tell us something?' said Dr Irvine. He set his coffee on the window ledge and left the room.

'Sell us something, more like,' said his wife to Brad. 'I wouldn't have one of them about the place.'

'One of what?' said Brad.

'Roman Catholics.'

Brad smiled and excused himself. He flicked his cigarette end into the fire and followed Dr Irvine out.

The two doctors went to the front door and down the steps. They waited for the little party to approach. By this time Peter was no longer clowning. He had transformed and become upright again. He held the two sticks up triumphantly.

'Well, who have we here?' said Brad.

'These are two of my girls,' said Peter. 'Finnoula and Rosaleen.'

'What lovely Irish names.'

'A complete pair of imps,' said their father. 'I've two more like them at home. Anne and Clare. These ones'd give you back cheek as quick as they'd look at you.' Being the centre of attention, the girls giggled and nudged each other. They had knitted scarves but no overcoats. 'It's a bit of luck to find you both together,' said Peter. 'We were going to traipse out to the camp to see *you*.' He nodded at Brad. 'Because I promised you sticks. And sticks you shall have.'

He held both blackthorns upright for the doctors to see.

'It was the girls' idea to decorate them. Difficult things to wrap, if you know what I mean.'

Around the neck of each was tied a twist of coloured wool. Maroon, navy, yellow. The handles were not right-angle bends, but in both cases were bunched fists. At the ground end, a bright ferrule cut from a metal pipe.

'These men saved your daddy's life,' Peter spoke to his children. But still the girls just pushed each other and laughed. Peter handed a stick to each man. The two doctors brandished and tested them.

'Good, eh? The way they fit the hand.'

'Great,' said Dr Irvine. He looked his stick over. Its varnished sheen, its dark nodules, the paleness of the handle, its different colours of wood. He turned to wave at the two women still in the window and motioned the stick, like he was beating them. The women laughed silently.

Brad said that he'd never remove the wool the girls had tied to his stick.

'Decorations that'll be there for ever,' he said. 'What are the sticks?'

'Blackthorn,' said Peter. Brad tested it for straightness with his eye, aiming it like a rifle. 'It's as straight as can be. I hang a boulder from them with twine – for about a year after they're cut – to straighten them. They're jagged and straight at the same time. So straight you could rule with them.'

Brad thanked Peter for his gift. Dr Irvine kept nodding and muttering, 'There was no need. It's very kind,' he said. 'You could get two, maybe three swagger sticks out of this one.'

He shortened the stick and tucked it up under his arm to demonstrate. The conversation seemed to die away and Dr Irvine began backing towards the house. When there was sufficient distance between them, he shouted his thanks for a final time and gestured to Brad to come into the porch. Both men waved goodbye with their sticks. Dr Irvine closed the door.

In the driveway Peter turned up the collar of his jacket and put his head down into the sleet, which was becoming heavier. It blew diagonally into their faces. He told the girls to tighten their scarves. Then he took each daughter and led them even-handedly out onto the main road.

ACKNOWLEDGEMENTS

For my daughter Claire who read these stories and reacted to them. I am in your debt.

For Anne Tannahill, friend and publisher, for your continual support and advice.

For Robin Robertson, editor since forever – thank you.

And I wish to acknowledge Scottish Book Trust's generous Robert Louis Stevenson fellowship at Grez-sur-Loing, France during June 2019 where I worked on this book.